The Relentless Shadow

by

Michael Limmer

Neal Gallian Trilogy, Book 2

'Though you search for your enemies, you shall not find them'.

Isaiah 41:12

This is a work of fiction, and accordingly parts of the city of Oxford and Oxfordshire countryside have been re-designed to fit the plot. All characters are drawn from the author's imagination and bear no relation to any persons living or dead.
It's fiction – enjoy it!

Mystery Thrillers from Michael Limmer

The Last Breath of Summer

Don't Start Now

A Heart to Betray

A Whisper in the Gloom

Past Deceiving

Marla

The Neal Gallian Trilogy

The Scars of Shame

The Relentless Shadow

All titles available in paperback and e-book via Amazon or from mike_limmer@yahoo.com

THE RELENTLESS SHADOW

PROLOGUE

He supposed the shadow would always be there, ready at any moment to enshroud him. Had there ever been a time when there'd not been a shadow of some kind?

He'd been an only child, lonely, his parents stuffed full of a dull religion which he'd never felt inspired to share. They'd gone their way some time ago, abandoning, rejecting him, leaving him alone.

From a boy he'd been alone, sullen, reclusive, never quite able to accept the hand of friendship when it was offered.

And when the suspicion of friendship loomed, it often heralded a false dawn. Somehow, in his naivety, he would be gulled, cheated. That time he'd been lured into gambling, into the promise of easy money which had turned inevitably sour, he'd been offered a loan to pay his debts and had found himself repaying far more than he could possibly earn, owing to spiralling interest charges imposed by people he wouldn't dare to mess with.

He'd turned to theft, small deceptions at first, but finally needing that last push to get his creditors off his back. His greatest mistake had been to buy the gun. He'd needed something to show that he was in control, that he wasn't afraid. He recalled the surge of power he'd felt as he'd threatened the shopkeeper with the gun, the man's face riddled with fear.

But he'd been afraid too, he always had been. He didn't intend to be caught, couldn't bear the thought of imprisonment, incarceration, knew he'd lose his reason if ever that occurred.

And in his haste to get away, he'd killed a man, wounded another. In total panic, he'd run, moved away, disguised himself, the beard helping to subdue his pale, haunted features. He'd found a job, worked hard at it, an escape route from his horrific past.

As if he could ever escape it. And he'd remained alone, always alone and always hiding, recalcitrant, lurking in the shadow.

Because there would always be the shadow…

March 1964

1

On a miserable afternoon in mid-March, Neal Gallian was standing in a corner of a ploughed field, hands in his raincoat pockets, grimacing in the steady rain. Water dripped languidly off the brim of his hat, and he felt its cold, tickling progress behind his shirt collar, drop after drop wriggling down his back.

He was glad he'd stashed a pair of wellingtons in the car boot because he was up to his ankles in squelching, glutinous mud and slowly sinking deeper.

The murmuring silhouettes in the flimsy, hastily erected tent at least enjoyed some sort of cover. Neal didn't envy their proximity to the grisly remains they were currently probing but supposed he'd have his turn viewing them once the pathologist had finished his examination back at the mortuary.

He had to admit that the job could have its downside, but for all that it could throw at him, Neal Gallian was a happy man.

Six months ago, he'd been recovering in a hospital bed, having been shot again in what he supposed he could say had been the line of duty. But on this occasion, even though he'd lost a lot of blood, the wound hadn't been so serious, and the consequences entirely different from the previous occasion. His life had morphed from negative to positive, thanks mainly to Jill Westmacott.

Jill's love for him and his for her had brought about a transformation in him. At Detective Chief Inspector Pilling's request or more likely at his insistence, knowing the Guv'nor, Neal had re-joined the police after an absence of almost two years. He was back at Oxford nick but no longer in uniform. Pilling had wanted him in CID, initially as a Detective Constable. Three months on, he'd found himself in the role of Acting Detective Sergeant, as Pilling's long-term sidekick, Len Thackray, had been taken ill and was signed off for the foreseeable future. The station's other DS, Phil Winter, had been seconded to the Met on making it to Detective

Inspector, so Neal had been offered a temporary promotion, and a new Detective Constable, whom he was yet to meet, had been drafted in a couple of days ago. It meant there was plenty to do, but Neal wasn't going to quarrel with that.

He'd recently moved out of his digs in South Oxford. He and Jill were planning to marry later in the year and, unknown to her, he'd obtained a mortgage on a flat in Headington. It'd be their first home and, on his days off, he'd begun to decorate and furnish it, hoping to present it to her on her return.

Jill was currently in Kenya, where her parents ran a school. Ben, her dad, had broken his leg, and Jill had gone out in early February to help her mum Janet with the teaching. She was due home at the weekend, and Neal was counting the hours because he'd missed her terribly, the sane, fixed point in his life. In the seven months since they'd met, she'd lifted him from a torpor of near despair. Two years previously, he'd been wounded in a shooting, his best friend and colleague killed, and he'd blamed himself for that, knowing that he could and should have reacted more quickly to save him. Once he'd recovered, Neal had turned his back on his police career, but events had taken a turn when, as a civilian, he'd become caught up in a mystery which had brought him back in contact with DCI Pilling and, above everything, had introduced Jill Westmacott into his life.

Neal stirred damply as a long, spare frame ducked out of the tent and approached him. Hubert Mather was the police surgeon, called in to confirm that the victim's life was extinct.

"Has been for some time," Mather said lugubriously. "And you won't have needed me to tell you that. Still, for the sake of form…"

"The farmer unearthed him when he was ploughing," Neal replied. "Told us he doesn't usually plough so close to the edge of the field." He grinned mirthlessly. "I imagine he wishes he hadn't this time. Anything you can tell me, Doc? Apart from the fact that he's dead?"

Mather shrugged. "As you know, you'll have to wait for the pathology boys to give you the full picture. The body's a bit mangled and getting ploughed up didn't help. He's a youngish male, shot twice in the chest, and one of the bullets is still in him. Whoever buried him had rolled him up in some old carpet, so he's not as badly chewed up as he might have been. I'd say he's been in the ground a while – we can give you a more accurate idea once we've examined him. Here, this might help identify him."

Mather held out what looked like a little booklet, dangling it from a corner between a gloved finger and thumb. Neal quickly slipped on disposable gloves and took it gently from him, recognising it as a driving licence.

"It had slipped down the lining of his windcheater," Mather explained. "There was nothing else on him. Whoever did this didn't want him identified, should the body ever have been found."

Neal carefully prised open the driving licence. "Anyone you know?" Mather asked.

"Derek Medway," Neal replied. "Yes, I know a bit about him. A local villain, into safe-breaking. He had some form. Thanks, Doc. I'd better report back to the DCI. I seem to recall Medway went missing a few years back, after committing a burglary. Doesn't look like he reaped any rewards from his crime."

"I'd say you're right, Sergeant. I'll make sure Pathology send the report through as soon as possible." He grinned sourly. "Knowing Don Pilling, he'll want it yesterday."

"If not sooner," Neal replied laconically.

*

Half-an-hour later, he was knocking on the DCI's office door to be met by a mumbled invitation to come in. Pilling's office was small and engulfed in clouds of smoke. As Neal waded in, he made out the familiar tin of Bondman on the desk and beyond it, slowly becoming visible through the haze, the figure of his boss drawing on a pipe.

"Ah, Neal. Sit down."

The use of his Christian name persuaded Neal that Don Pilling was in a mellow mood, something which wasn't always the case. He was a wiry individual in his mid- to late forties, sharp, relentless eyes peering out from beneath thick, dark brows. He sat in shirtsleeves, his tie askew and jacket slung over the back of his chair, a mountain of paperwork on the desk before him. He'd been instrumental in Neal re-joining the force, having previously been impressed by his capacity for work. Pilling was a hard taskmaster, strict, direct but never unfair, and what appealed to Neal was that you always knew where you stood with him.

"The ploughed-up corpse, I take it? Anyone we know?"

"Driving licence in his jacket lining helped us there, Guv. And you'll like this: Derek Medway."

Pilling took that in. Neal could tell he was pleased, because he went as far as resting the pipe in his ashtray.

"So, he's turned up at last. Any idea how long he's been there?"

"Doc Mather reckons a while. Pathology are on to it and will send you their report. I said you'd want it given priority."

The DCI nodded curtly. "Oh, you bet I do. Remember Medway, do you?"

"It all happened a few months before I was put out of action. Fancied himself as a safebreaker, didn't he? But something went wrong. Some art dealer's house that he broke into – and wasn't a man killed?"

Another nod. "That's the one. And it's a long story. Should be a file in the top drawer of that cabinet behind you. I like to keep the unsolved cases near to hand and mull over them from time to time." His thin face twitched with an unscheduled grin. "This won't mean case closed, of course. Someone must have shot Medway and buried him in that field."

Neal got up and looked out the relevant folder, passing it to his boss, who picked up and deployed his pipe again while he leafed through it.

"Ah, here we are. The break-in took place on Wednesday 22nd November '61."

Neal nodded grimly. *Three months before **it** happened.* He recalled how much he'd enjoyed his time in uniform, driving the squad cars, how he'd planned to sit his sergeant's exams in the coming months. It had been good until things had got complicated, until the car chase which had ended at the warehouse near the Oxpens, and the gunshots which had changed his life…

"Bernard Ellison, 59, a reputable art dealer with a gallery and house in North Oxford," Pilling summarised. "His wife told us he'd had a good sale the previous week, a painting sold for cash. Some French daub…"

"I seem to recall it was a Monet," Neal put in, withholding a grin.

"I'll take your word for it. Anyway, the sale was reported in the *Mail,* and our Derek saw it. Couldn't have occurred to him that Ellison would already have banked most of the money. He must have waited outside the house and watched their car drive off. But there was only Mrs Ellison in it, on her way to some *soirée* at a friend's house – all which checked out, by the way.

"Once she'd gone, Medway jemmied the French window round the back of the gallery, got in and set to work on the safe. Couldn't have given him much difficulty because he had time to sample Ellison's best malt whisky. He got careless – left his fingerprints on the glass and bottle, even though he'd remembered to wipe the safe clean. Probably got out in a hurry, though, because Ellison disturbed him, and Medway did him in with a poker before making off…"

"Doesn't sound the most successful villain, guv."

"He wasn't. He'd had a couple of previous convictions but simply couldn't go straight. It was usual for him to operate alone, although I always wondered if he'd had an accomplice, someone who'd perhaps put him up to it without realising there wasn't a vast amount of money in the safe, nor that Mrs Ellison's jewellery was kept locked away in the bedroom."

He handed across Derek Medway's photograph. He'd been in his mid-thirties, close-cropped fair hair, thickset and not looking the brightest star in the galaxy.

"Think you'd be right about the accomplice, Guv. Oh, and the doc said he'd been shot twice and that one of the bullets was still in him. Ballistics will get back on that."

"Hhmm, interesting. Sounds like whoever did away with him was seriously narked by his lack of success and wanted to distance himself from Ellison's murder. Once caught, they'd both have swung for it."

"Any ideas at the time?" Neal asked.

Pilling looked sour as he puffed away at his pipe. "We hauled in his friends and acquaintances, but I'm satisfied that none of them were involved. Mrs Ellison wondered if it might have been someone her husband knew, but it was tenuous. Only glimmer we had was from a telephone conversation Medway's mum overheard. She runs the Carpenter's Arms off the Cowley Road and, whenever he wasn't doing time, Derek helped out behind the bar. Day before it happened, she overheard him on the blower saying something like "we'll come to some arrangement". He put down the phone pretty quickly when he realized she was close by and clammed up when she asked what it was all about."

"I'll need to get in touch with her," Neal said. "Take her along to identify the body and find out if there's anything else she can tell us."

The DCI looked doubtful. "We covered all the ground and more at the time, Neal. Alerted all ports and airports in case Medway tried leaving the country. Every inquiry led nowhere. He just – disappeared. Now, at last, we know why."

He reached across, picked up and shuffled a few papers. "Well, I'll leave that one in your capable hands. I'll let you know when Pathology and Ballistics report back, see where we go from there. You'd better get back to your decorating. Your young lady's due home soon, isn't she?"

Neal felt surprised and gratified that his boss was taking an interest in something other than work. He knew the DCI's wife gave him a hard time over the number of hours he spent out of the house, although given the volume of paperwork piled on his desk, Neal could see why.

"Back Saturday afternoon," he replied. "I'm fetching her from London Airport. And yes, some way to go on the decorating, although she doesn't know about the flat yet. I hope she'll like it."

He wished Pilling good evening and went out to his car. He was looking forward to Saturday, but before he got there, he'd have the small matter of confirming the identity of the remains which had turned up in that muddy field.

Something else to look forward to.

2

The next morning was fittingly grey and cold for the task which lay ahead of him, as Neal rapped on the door of the Carpenter's Arms, a pub in a narrow street of terraced houses, just off the Cowley Road. He'd brought a WPC with him, Yvonne Begley, experienced at dealing with the bereaved after more than ten years with the force. Although he guessed that where Doris Medway was concerned, Yvonne might be surplus to requirements.

Doris answered the door immediately, a short, pugnacious figure in a grey mackintosh with a silk scarf over her head. She grunted a greeting as Neal introduced himself before opening the car's rear door and ushering her in alongside Yvonne. No-one spoke as they drove across Oxford to the mortuary.

The building was typically uninviting, grim and sanitized, and their plodding footsteps echoed alarmingly in the bare corridors, Doris following behind him, her gaze set fixedly ahead.

They were met by an attendant and led into a room where a body covered by a white sheet lay on a gurney. Neal stood slightly behind Doris as the attendant lifted a corner of the sheet, although he thought he'd be the more likely of the two of them to faint. Viewing corpses didn't rate highly on his list of favourite occupations. He withheld a grin as he recalled a previous occasion as a young constable, when Don Pilling had congratulated him on being one of the few in his experience not to throw up or pass out at the sight of a mangled corpse, Pilling counting himself among the failures. Neal had replied that it had been a close-run thing. It still was.

"That's him," Doris Medway said, after the first shocked moment. "That's my son – Derek Medway."

Neal allowed his gaze to fall on the man's face, pale and untroubled in the repose of death. The mortuary staff had made a good job of cleaning him up, and Neal recognised Medway from having questioned him on some matter years before.

He thanked the attendant and nodded to Yvonne, who moved up alongside Doris and steered her towards the door. "Are you alright, Mrs Medway?" she inquired solicitously.

"I think so, dear," Doris replied. "Could do with a cup of tea, though."

"Shall we take you back home?" Neal suggested. "There are a few questions I'd like to ask."

"Thought you might," Doris said. "How did Derek die, Mr Gallian?"

"I'm afraid he was shot."

The woman sighed, stumbled a little, her first sign of weakness, and Yvonne caught hold of her arm and steadied her.

"Ah, I see. Poor lad. Poor, daft lad."

The Carpenter's Arms was a small, no-frills public house, with a tap room and snug either side of a flagged passageway which led down to Doris's living quarters at the rear of the building. The room was cluttered with armchairs, a small dining table, and faded prints ranged around the drab walls. Yvonne went through to the little scullery to make some tea and soon had the kettle singing away. Doris's husband, Norman, had run the pub but had died of a heart attack some five years previously. She'd taken it on, alongside some local help behind the bar. It was a hard life, made more so by the uncertainty of what had happened to her son, a cloud which had hung over her for more than two years.

She sighed as Yvonne handed her a mug of strong tea. "S'pose it's something of a relief. I never thought our Derek would just have scarpered without getting in touch in some way." She fixed Neal with a hard stare. "I can assure you he wouldn't have been in this alone, Mr Gallian. Someone was in it with him – I said so before and I say it again now, partic'ly after the bloke have gone and shot him dead."

It was Neal's opinion too. Medway couldn't have known how little money there would have been in Bernard Ellison's safe. He imagined Medway and his accomplice quarrelling, coming to blows, then worse than blows…

"I thought he'd gone straight after that last stretch," Doris went on. "He promised his dad on his deathbed that he'd settle down and help me run this place. 'Course, I never knew what he got up to on his evenings off. Obviously up to no good. And they were a motley crew he hung about with."

"Any idea who these friends of his were, Mrs Medway?"

Doris shook her head, her expression sour. "No-one who came in here. Any of his dodgy mates happened in, I'd show 'em the door. Several of 'em weren't welcome, as in not at all - Arnold Skelton and that sly little devil Rudd to name but two. If he wanted to meet up with any of them, it had to be away from here." Her features softened, and Neal saw the beginnings of tears in her eyes. "I'll tell you this now, Mr Gallian. I told 'em back when Derek went missing, and I'll say it again: he was a bad lot, always was, from school. Sly, dishonest. A cheat. Oh, Norman used to larrup him something awful, if he found out he'd been stealing. It never cured him. Took too much after my younger brother, who was killed in the war. But I'd swear on my mother's grave that our Derek was no killer. I don't care what anyone says: he'd never have brained that poor man with a poker."

"The evidence goes against that, I'm afraid, Mrs Medway." Neal tried to inject some sympathy into his words, particularly as Doris was looking as if she might make an issue of it. But of course, their thinking up to the previous day had been that Derek had done a runner. He hadn't. And someone had murdered him. It opened up the likelihood of an accomplice and would need looking into.

He tried another tack. "Mrs Medway, you said at the time that you overheard Derek making a phone call the night before the burglary?"

"Yes, I was crossing between the tap room and snug, and he was on the blower in the passageway there. I heard him say clearly, "We can come to some arrangement." Then he realized I was there and clammed up, said something like "I'll be in touch" and put down the phone."

"He gave no indication as to whom he was calling?"

Doris shook her head glumly. "None. 'Course, it might have been the bloke he was planning it with, the bloke who – oh, dear Lord - did that to him…" Her hand sped to her mouth. Neal deliberately pressed on.

"And on the Wednesday?"

"He went off halfway through the evening – often did when he should've been helping me, and that made it twice that week. He'd been out on the Monday with his mates, boozing 'til all hours I shouldn't wonder. The Wednesday night he'd smartened himself up some. Had on a windcheater over a shirt and grey flannels, and some black slip-on shoes he'd not long bought off the market. I did wonder if he was meeting some woman – though what type she'd have been I shudder to think."

Neal nodded. Doris had just described the clothes Derek Medway had been dug up in.

Doris shrugged hopelessly. "So, nothing new, Mr Gallian. Everything's just as I told it to your man who came to see me at the time. Tubby bloke, fair bit shorter 'n you."

Neal grinned. "I know who you mean." *Detective Constable Mal Brady*. Neal would shortly have a job for him, re-interviewing Derek Medway's list of questionable acquaintances. Brady would be sure to have something to say about that, probably along the lines of 'I already did that once.'

Like it or not, he'd soon be doing it again.

*

Neal's next call, once he'd dropped Yvonne Begley back at the station, was by way of contrast to the little working-class pub he'd just left: a large, detached house in a North Oxford cul-de-sac, which screamed money at him. It had swallowed up what he assumed had once been Bernard Ellison's gallery, now converted into a spacious dining room with a rectangular oak table surrounded with high-backed chairs, and long pastel-green velvet drapes at the French windows.

He pulled round on the gravelled drive to bring the dark blue unmarked police Anglia up behind a gleaming white, new-looking Ford Cortina. Farther along, outside the double garage, stood a sedate little Austin A40. He guessed that belonged to Mrs Ellison and the Cortina to a visitor. He made a wager with himself that the visitor was male. After all, Ellison had been dead for well over two years, and his widow, according to Taff Thomas who'd been involved with the original inquiry, a bit of a stunner.

She opened the door to him, a pleasant-faced woman somewhere in her forties, tastefully made up, light-brown hair in a bouffant style and dressed elegantly in a chunky sweater and tight grey skirt.

"Mrs Ellison? Acting Detective Sergeant Neal Gallian, Oxford CID." He waved his warrant card vaguely towards her.

"Oh? And what can I do for you, Sergeant?"

"It concerns your late husband, madam." He hesitated briefly, as she seemed to show no inclination to let him in, then lowered his voice, although there was no-one remotely within eavesdropping range. "I think we may have found his killer."

As he'd hoped, that registered with her, although not to any great extent.

"Ah, I see. Perhaps you'd better come in."

She shifted a little to let him pass, closed the door and led him down a long, carpeted hallway to where double doors stood open on to a wide, airy lounge. The drapes which hung either side of the bay window were similar to those in the other room, and the furniture, two sofas and three armchairs in white leather, looked as though they'd never been sat upon. Over against the far wall stood a radiogram in a highly polished dark wood, and a man stood over it, his back to the door, flicking through a handful of LP sleeves. Neal noticed Perry Como, Jim Reeves and Frank Sinatra among the selection: obviously Mrs Ellison was into easy listening. Easy living, too, he guessed, as he quickly surveyed the room.

The man turned on hearing them enter. He looked slim and dapper in a light grey suit, dark blue shirt and white tie. His neat brown shoes with white stitching looked Italian and expensive, if a little flashy. Neal put him at around forty, trying and almost succeeding in looking thirty.

"Who's this, Nadine?" he inquired lightly.

"A policeman, Dale. He's got some news."

The man wandered over and stretched out a hand, his smile perfunctory and impossibly white. "Dale Corlett."

As he shook it, Neal caught a pungent whiff of cologne which put his Old Spice firmly in the shade. "Neal Gallian, Oxford CID."

Corlett didn't look as if he'd make any effort to leave the room, and Nadine Ellison sensed Neal's hesitation.

"Oh, it's alright, Sergeant. I'm happy for Dale to hear this. He's a good friend."

Neal didn't doubt it. As Corlett moved forward to stand supportively beside Nadine, Neal noticed he was slightly shorter than her, even given that she was wearing low-heeled shoes. He also realised that he was distrustful of the man: there seemed to be something almost predatory about him.

Nadine invited him to sit, and Neal took an armchair, while she sat across from him on one of the sofas. Corlett moved round to stand behind her, an invigilating presence.

"So, Sergeant. You've finally found Bernard's killer? I suppose it's that man – what was his name? Midway?"

"Derek Medway."

"And you've arrested and charged him?"

"That won't be possible, Mrs Ellison." Neal paused long enough for Corlett, as he'd somehow expected, to look affronted and open his mouth to protest on his lady friend's behalf. "You see," he went on, "he was dead, and we're waiting on the pathologist to inform us how long that's been the case."

"Dead?" Nadine's surprise was to be expected. "But – how did he die?"

"As you know, he disappeared immediately after the break-in, leaving some fingerprints on a glass and a bottle. Into thin air, it seemed, and we're thinking he may have had an accomplice, possibly the man who shot him. My guess is that Medway died soon after the break-in."

"Then that's it, is it? Case closed?"

"In one respect. But we still need to find the person who shot Medway, and the accomplice – unless they're one and the same man."

Nadine Ellison shrugged in a superior way. "But that's no concern of mine, Sergeant. It's a pity this man Medway cheated the gallows, but really, for me, it's all over now."

"And that must be such a relief for you, Nadine," Corlett gushed. Neal thought he'd have to put in his twopenn'orth before long, an attempt to further insinuate himself into her good graces.

"It is Dale, certainly." She patted the hand which had strayed to rest on her shoulder. *Good dog,* Neal thought viciously. No, he really didn't like Corlett.

He got to his feet. The leather cushion had been firm, but he preferred the unfussy little G-plan two-seater he'd recently purchased for his flat.

"That's it, really, Mrs Ellison. Just wanted to keep you up to date."

Nadine rose too, smiling graciously. "And I appreciate that, Sergeant." She began to lead off towards the door. He and Corlett nodded their goodbyes, and the latter returned to the LPs over by the radiogram.

"You didn't continue with the gallery, then?" Neal observed, as he followed her down the hallway.

"Oh, Bernard was the art expert." She indicated several paintings lining the hallway and stairs. Impressionists, Neal guessed, delving into his limited knowledge of art. "I kept one or two pieces, in his memory. No, I'm in the fashion business myself. Do you know *Lady Luck* in Queen Street?"

"That's yours?" It was pricey, for certain. He recalled Jill buying an outfit there with some money her uncle had given her for Christmas.

"Yes, I started it up and oversee the buying and accounting. I've a competent manageress in place, so don't need to spend every day there myself."

They'd reached the door, and Neal smiled and offered a hand. Nadine's grip was light and cool, detached and superior like the house, like its owner.

"I'll be in touch when there's anything more to report, Mrs Ellison," he promised.

"Thank you, Sergeant. And thank you for calling. Poor Bernard. But I suppose in a way justice has been served. And at least that man didn't benefit from his crime."

Her words held a hint of closure, and Neal sensed that she was ready to move on.

And that possibly she'd moved on some time ago.

3

It was afternoon by the time Neal had settled to some paperwork in his office. Technically, the office wasn't his, as it had housed Phil Winter, a young, ambitious detective, who'd made it to DI before being seconded to the Met. Neal had never met him, as he'd turned his back on the force before Winter had arrived in Oxford. The office was smaller than Pilling's, though less congested, and would have been smaller still if Winter had remained in residence, because Neal would have had to take the desk pushed up against the far wall, which had been Len Thackray's.

He was finishing a report which he'd ask one of the WPCs to type up, when there came a knock on the door, and PC Taff Thomas stuck his head round. "DCI's asking to see you, Gally," he announced briskly.

"What, as of now?" Neal hadn't long left him, having looked in to report on his two calls that morning.

Thomas grinned. "You know the DCI."

Neal returned the grin, because it had been a stupid question in the first place, pushed back his chair and followed him out into the corridor. He noticed that Taff was making his way back to the duty officer's desk and guessed that Tom Wrightson, the usual incumbent, must be out on a call.

He walked the few paces to Pilling's office, knocked and was summoned inside. The DCI sat at his desk, thankfully with his pipe redundant in an ashtray.

Beside the desk sat Tom Wrightson, the duty sergeant. 'Uncle Tom', as the station knew him, was a bald, broad-shouldered Yorkshireman, who was all encouragement to the workers and came down heavily on anyone who didn't pull their weight. Along with Pilling, he'd played his part in persuading Neal to return to the force. He and the DCI were about the same age, had worked together for years and rubbed along well.

Although at that moment in time, both men were looking somewhat po-faced, and Neal wondered if he was about to be hauled over the coals for some misdemeanour.

"Ah, Neal, take a seat." He did so, relieved, because his boss wouldn't have used his Christian name if he supposed him to have done anything wrong.

Pilling lifted a sheet of paper off the desk. "Pathology report," he announced curtly. "Derek Medway's been dead for at least two years. He was wearing the clothes his mother had last seen him in, so it suggests he was topped soon after the break-in." He shoved the paper dismissively into a tray. "Doesn't tell us anything we hadn't already guessed."

He picked up a second sheet of paper, held it in both hands and leaned forward purposefully, his elbows resting on the desk.

"However, this is different. It's from Ballistics." Pilling was gazing at Neal intently from beneath his thick, dark brows. "Seems as if the gun was an Enfield No. 2 revolver, a type issued to the British Army in the war. A common enough weapon." He paused weightily. "But here's what's so interesting - the bullet in Medway came from the same gun used on you and Clyde Holt two years ago."

Neal's face must have been a study in astonishment. He'd not been back there for a while, too busy to be haunted by the nightmare he'd relived so often. Pilling's words crashed into him with all the force of the bullet which had sent him reeling back into the piles of boxes in the warehouse, and he found himself reliving the shock, the pain as it had ripped into his flesh, his collapse to the floor and the spiralling whirl through shadowy, half-remembered images into oblivion.

He could almost feel that pain again; the pain, too, more lasting and devastating, of that hideous past reclaiming him. He'd thought to be embarking on a new phase of life: his enthusiastic return to the job, an unlooked-for if temporary promotion, the enticing prospect of sharing a future with Jill. Instead, he found himself plunged back into that morass of obligation: back to the debt he owed Clyde Holt, to track down his best friend's killer, to atone in some small way for his abject failure to save him.

His response to Pilling's words was feeble, his voice small and wavering. "But – but are they *sure?*"

"Some young egghead in Ballistics probably out to impress his boss with his dedication, but yes, he's come up with the goods, and there seems to be no mistake. The striations on the bullet are a match with the earlier ones."

"Then if it's the same gun, might it be the same man who pulled the trigger?"

The words limped out, an amazed, impulsive reaction: he still couldn't think straight and immediately quashed the idea himself. "But no, that doesn't follow, does it?"

"Not necessarily," the DCI replied levelly. "But it has to be borne in mind that Medway died a good three months before the shooting at the warehouse."

Pilling was watching him closely, and when he spoke again his voice was stern. "Alright, DS Gallian, I want you to investigate this. But I have to know if you feel up to it."

Neal didn't answer immediately, needing time to reflect. There'd been a time, not so long ago, when he'd have charged into this with all guns blazing. Now, he had responsibilities. His boss had referred to him as 'DS Gallian'. Pilling had never used the adjective 'Acting' in Neal's hearing. The DCI had put his faith in him to carry out a difficult job, previously and for years done competently by the incapacitated Len Thackray. If Len didn't return to work, Pilling would expect Neal to grasp the opportunity offered. And Neal was very much in his boss's debt.

Then there was Jill. Later in the year, he'd make his marriage vows and would in no way take them lightly: *to have and to hold from this day forth*. He was fully committed to that, because her love for him had turned his life around.

He thought briefly about the man he'd be seeking. He'd never been able to find out anything about him. Privately, he referred to him as 'The Face', because all he'd had had been a fleeting glimpse of a man's pale, terrified features through the warehouse's open window. The face of Clyde Holt's killer.

Could he find him now? The man had had no police record. Neal had searched through the files time and again, and in vain. He accepted the conclusion that the man hadn't been local. The van he'd used had been stolen, and he'd worn gloves, as there'd been no fresh prints on the steering wheel or door. So, someone just passing through? On his way to where, and from where? If anyone had known him, they were keeping quiet to protect his identity, because no-one had come forward, there'd been no leads at all.

Could that be about to change? Because now, if he could track down the gun which had been used to kill Derek Medway, might it lead him to the Face?

At last, he looked up and gave his response, noticing the concern in the expressions of both Pilling and Tom Wrightson.

"Yes, Guv," he said. "Yes. I want this."

Pilling's answer was to switch a glance at the man who sat beside him. "Tom?"

Wrightson's steady gaze locked with Neal's own. "I'd back Neal on this, sir."

Neal acknowledged Tom's support with a nod. Don Pilling's own dour nod towards him constituted permission to go ahead.

"Much as I value Tom's input," he went on, "I didn't call him in just for a character reference." He indicated for Tom to speak.

The sergeant tapped a folder on the desk beside him. "There could be another line of inquiry here, lad. We investigated it at the time, and I was involved with some of the questioning. But we came to a dead end – another of those unsolved cases.

"There was a series of hold-ups in Oxford during late '61 and early '62. Nothing major by any means. All the reports and statements are in here. It was one man with a gun, targeting corner shops in the evenings. No rich pickings for certain, and no violence either. The shopkeeper in there alone, and our friend was quickly in and out, taking the contents of the till with him. He wore a balaclava, but all the victims agree he had the bearing of a young man.

"One shopkeeper recognised the make of the gun: a wartime Enfield No. 2. As soon as the Guv'nor mentioned this afternoon about the bullets matching in both cases, I thought back to this. It's a very long punt, I admit. But could it be the same gun in all three cases – and maybe the same man?

"And here's something else to ponder. An Enfield revolver was reported stolen in late October '61 by a Major Roger Peaching – his address is in the folder. He was fairly local and is still there according to the phone directory. It's the only theft of an Enfield we've a record of. It may mean something – or nothing at all. That type of revolver was very common. There must be hundreds of them knocking around, and the gun used didn't have to have been stolen. Still, it'll give you a starting point, only don't set your hopes too high."

Neal took Tom Wrightson's warning on board, but he'd already made his decision. He was backed by two experienced officers for whom he had the greatest respect, and this time he wasn't slow to respond.

"I'm going to need some help with this, Guv. There are interviews to revisit regarding the hold-ups and a number of Medway's acquaintances that we saw at the time. We've talked about the likelihood of Medway having had an accomplice. That's an important angle: who killed Medway, and was his killer in on the break-in and the murder of Bernard Ellison?"

"You're right, Neal," Pilling replied. "I'm sure we could spare a couple of bods to help you, eh, Tom?" He grinned, an unusual occurrence, and shared it with Wrightson.

"Aye, sir, I dare say. Who did you have in mind? Our new recruit?"

"Yes – Dakers. Perhaps DC Brady as well?"

"We can always spare him," Tom mumbled darkly.

Pilling turned back to Neal. "Brady was in on the original investigation into Medway's disappearance," he said. "So, you might as well brief him now, set him to work and keep him at it. Young Dakers has been out with one of our squad cars these last couple of days, getting acquainted with the lie of the land. Once you've sorted Brady, Neal, you might as well call it a day – I know it's a busy weekend for you – and crack on with all this first thing Monday."

Neal agreed to that, got up, thanked them both and left the office. He had much to ponder. He'd shown both men a positive attitude. It was up to him to maintain that, not let his feelings get the better of him. And if the gun used in the hold-ups wasn't the weapon he was seeking, then to admit it and move on. It would do no good trying to wring something from a case that was dead in the water.

As chance would have it, he came across DC Brady in the corridor, Brady overweight and scruffy in shirtsleeves, rumpled trousers and a tie seriously askew.

"Oh, Mal, got a minute?"

"Just on my way for a cuppa, Gally. Will it keep?"

"Not really. Come in. This won't take long. I've got a job for you and just want to outline it so that you can make an early start on it on Monday."

"Oh, right." Brady looked underwhelmed. "Hope it's something decent?"

"You'll love it."

4

The first thing Neal did on reaching the flat was to phone Jill's uncle, Lambert Wilkie, a retired army colonel, at his home near Braxbury, a small market town some twenty miles west of Oxford, in case it had slipped his mind that his niece would be returning to England the following day.

"Ah, thank you, my boy. I hadn't forgotten. Indeed, I'd written myself a note to pop along to the butcher's tomorrow morning for a joint of beef for Sunday lunch. Suppose I'd better have a tidy round too, or else I'll be in trouble."

"I can come over in the morning and lend a hand if you like? Jill's flight's not due in until mid-afternoon."

"Would you, Neal?" The relief in Wilkie's voice was plain. "That'd be a great help. I fear housekeeping's not my forte."

Neal chuckled softly at the admission. He'd called on Wilkie a fortnight previously and had been astounded by the amount of detritus in and around the kitchen sink, as well as the haphazard state of the sitting room, with books and newspapers littering every surface. The colonel's particular glory-hole was the summerhouse in the back garden, recently rebuilt after a fire the previous year, and Neal supposed that throughout the cold winter he'd transferred most of his time and paperwork to the house. The colonel was writing his memoirs, a task which had been ongoing for some time.

Neal arranged to call on Wilkie early on, as he'd need to leave for London Airport soon after midday.

"And you'll join us for Sunday lunch, of course?" Wilkie invited.

"Thank you, Colonel. I'd love to."

He liked Wilkie, a straightforward, blunt yet compassionate former commanding officer but felt awkward about addressing him by his Christian name – something he'd never yet done. Neither did he think he'd ever address him as 'Uncle Lam', as Jill did. The very idea!

Neal was about to ring off when he was ambushed by a sudden thought.

"Oh, Colonel, before you go. You wouldn't happen to know a Major Roger Peaching? He lives out near Islip."

"Indeed, I do, Neal. We're old friends, hailing from the same regiment. Why do you ask?"

"I believe he reported some items stolen from him, more than two years ago now?"

Wilkie laughed good-naturedly. "Oh, don't I know it, my boy. We meet up for a chinwag from time to time, and poor old Peach is still harping on about it."

"Apparently one of the stolen items was a revolver, and it may well have featured in a case I'm looking into at the moment."

"I see. I take it you'll be wanting to call on him at some point. If so, I could get him to pop along here in the morning – save you a journey. I'm sure you've plenty going on in the criminal world to fill your time."

Neal gratefully accepted the offer. He'd only be going over old ground with Peaching, and to see him the next day would enable him to move the investigation on a little quicker on Monday. That was, he warned himself, if there was anything to investigate. As he'd already been reminded, Peaching's gun might not be the one in question.

"Yes, it'll be good to see the old duffer again," Wilkie concluded, "if only to commiserate over the way our boys are performing in the Five Nations."

*

Neal showed up early the next morning as promised and immediately pitched into the mountain of washing-up, setting Wilkie the task of tidying the sitting room and running the vacuum cleaner over the carpet. Once he'd finished in the kitchen, he went outside, cleaned the windows and chopped some wood for kindling. The nights could be cold, and the open fire downstairs was the sole form of heating in the old house. He guessed Jill would appreciate the central heating in their flat.

Neal worked busily away, spurred on by fond memories of carrying out similar chores when he'd lodged with Flo and Ron Ormsby on starting with the force in Cirencester. Indeed, he realised he'd been occupied for close on two hours when Wilkie called him in for coffee.

He'd heard the crunch of car tyres on the gravel drive a few minutes previously and guessed Major Peaching had arrived. He went in to find the two men comfortably ensconced in armchairs, the smoke from their pipes fogging the room and a large tin of Gold Block and a couple of ashtrays on the coffee table before them. Neal noticed with a wry smile that the vacuum cleaner was parked up in a corner of the room and very little tidying seemed to have been done. It was also left to him to fetch the tray containing the cups and coffee pot from the kitchen. "Oh, would you, Neal? Good man."

The colonel introduced Peaching, balding, tweed-suited and upright with military bearing, who stood to shake Neal's hand.

"And this is Detective Sergeant Neal Gallian, Oxford CID," Wilkie added, not bothering with the 'Acting' prefix – in common with DCI Pilling, he never did. "He also happens to be engaged to my niece Jill, whom you've met on previous occasions."

"Wilkie said you wanted a word, DS Gallian?" Peaching said, as he resumed his seat, and Neal poured and handed round the coffee. "What's happened? Has that revolver of mine turned up at last, by any chance?"

"Not quite, sir," Neal replied, as he eased himself down into one of Wilkie's ancient armchairs. "But a case I'm currently investigating involves an Enfield No.2. It may or may not turn out to be yours, but I'm trying to track it down. Would you mind talking me through the details of the robbery again? It's all down here in the file from when you were interviewed previously. But I'd like to double-check it, as I didn't take part in the original inquiry."

"A pleasure, Sergeant," Peaching said briskly. "Happy to be of service. I'd employed the little blighter as a gardener and handyman, as my usual chap had had to call it a day, and I can't say I trusted him from the outset. Made all the right noises, but I decided I'd need to keep an eye on him."

"This would be Arnold Skelton?"

"Skelton. Yes, that's the chap."

Neal knew Arnie Skelton, for their paths had crossed on a couple of occasions. He'd gone down for a few months once he'd been apprehended but was now supposed to be going straight. Neal believed Skelton was currently employed in Oxford's Covered Market and would look him up on Monday.

"And you realised things had gone missing around the end of the October, Major?"

"Items had been disappearing for a while, I believe, but I only tumbled to it when I missed my revolver, which had been issued to me by the Army at the beginning of the war. I became suspicious, because I knew exactly where I'd left it just a day or two before. I checked carefully round the house and discovered that certain items belonging to my late mother – valuable items of jewellery – were missing from their case."

"Did you approach Skelton about their disappearance?"

"I didn't get the chance. The little weasel hadn't shown up for work that morning – Monday 30th October, as I recall – and hadn't bothered to phone in. I immediately contacted your chaps, and I'm happy to say they picked up Skelton pretty quickly. I believe the jewellery proved his downfall." Peaching allowed himself a broad grin. "So, my dear old mater did for him after all. She never was one to suffer fools gladly."

There was no flaw in the Major's memory. He'd reported the theft on the 30th, as he'd said, and Arnie Skelton was picked up the next day trying to offload the jewellery at a pawnbroker's shop. His twitchy behaviour – cool and calm had never been part of Arnie's demeanour – had made the owner suspicious, and he'd immediately notified the police.

"All the jewellery was recovered," Peaching went on, "but sadly my old Enfield disappeared without trace. Had a certain sentimental value for me – oh, and hanging on to it after the war was all legal and above board, I assure you. Skelton reckoned it had been stolen from him – poetic justice if ever there was. I don't suppose you've any idea where it might have ended up, Sergeant?"

"I can only repeat that it may feature in my current investigation, Major. Sadly, I'm unable to give you any more details. I'm grateful for your help, however, and if and when there's more to report, I'll be in touch. I can assure you, though, I shall be interviewing our friend Skelton before long."

Neal didn't altogether buy Arnie Skelton's story of his loss of the revolver. Len Thackray had initially interviewed him, and Arnie had told him he'd been touting the gun to a group of men in an Oxford pub, didn't know their names and hadn't managed to interest them in making the purchase.

He'd been set upon after he'd left the pub, and the gun and his money taken from him. Thackray had noted that Skelton had a bruise on his left cheek, which looked as though someone had hit him, but when asked to describe the men he'd met in the pub, he'd been deliberately vague, and the pub landlord, who knew Arnie, wouldn't swear to having seen him in there on the evening in question. Neal knew he'd be pressing Skelton further on the matter.

He sat with the two army veterans as they finished their coffee, all of them bemoaning the fact that the England rugby team seemed currently off the pace in the Five Nations, and that it was likely to be a two-horse race for the Championship between Wales and Scotland.

As Wilkie and Peaching smoked and chatted on, Neal finished off his round of chores and doubted the colonel would finish off what he was supposed to be doing with the vacuum cleaner. Thanking them both again, he took his leave. He headed home for a quick bite to eat before setting off for London Airport and his long-awaited reunion with Jill.

Arnie Skelton could wait until Monday.

5

Neal started out in good time, anticipating a lot of traffic on the A40 towards London. Parking at the airport proved difficult, but fortunately Jill's flight was behind schedule. When it touched down, he joined the long line of people awaiting the arrivals, craning forward to catch a first glimpse of Jill's slight, girlish figure.

He almost missed her, face partially obscured by a floppy hat as she toiled along with a heavy suitcase. Muttering apologies to the people around him, he shouldered his way into the aisle. "Jill!"

She looked up, saw him, abandoned her suitcase and flew into his waiting arms. He gathered her up and whirled her round and, as her face closed in on his, succeeded in dislodging her hat and sending her glasses comically awry. Placing her back on her feet, he removed the glasses and drew her into a long, delicious kiss.

Finally, they paused for breath. "Oh, Neal darling, how I've missed you!"

"What, more than I've missed you? I didn't think that could be possible."

They stood glued together for glorious minutes, vaguely aware of the thumbs-up gestures and indulgent smiles from passers-by. He handed back her glasses, and Jill, putting them on, looked quickly around at the throng of passing passengers, meeters and greeters. "Oh, Lord! Have I made an exhibition of myself?" She was blushing, still the same, tentative, easily embarrassed Jill. And he wouldn't change her for the world.

"I believe I was involved too and equally guilty," Neal reassured her easily. "But who cares? I don't."

She smiled broadly. "Me neither."

Neal reached across and retrieved her suitcase. "Have you eaten?" he asked.

"I had something a while back on the flight, but I'd love a cup of tea and perhaps a sandwich."

They made their way across the concourse to a café, Jill hanging on to one of his arms and her suitcase occupying the other. He couldn't stop her chattering – not that he wanted to.

Her dad was on the mend and looking forward to resuming his teaching duties. Mum and Dad were coming over at the end of the summer for a holiday and, of course, the wedding. When they'd met Neal at Christmas, they'd liked him very much and couldn't wait to see him again in the summer. (Neal recalled the stuttering request he'd made of Ben Westmacott when he'd asked his permission for his daughter's hand. He liked Ben too and felt they'd have a lot in common).

Oh, and Mum and Dad had asked about the wedding list, so Jill would have to see what was needed, and how had Uncle Lam been coping alone? Oh dear, the house was bound to be in an *awful* mess, and did I tell you when I phoned last week that I've asked my cousin to be bridesmaid? Her name's Ella, she's a bit younger than me, but she was *thrilled,* and you'll really like her…

Neal listened on, smiling indulgently, lost in her already. He placed a hand over hers. "Draw breath, darling. Finish your tea. Your uncle's in good form and can't wait to see you. But we're stopping off before we reach Briar Hedge. I've a surprise for you."

Jill was immediately intrigued, and the flow of chatter ceased. "Oh? What kind of surprise?"

"I want to show you where I'm living now."

"Well, that's good news in itself, because it must mean you're no longer at Mrs Pendle's."

"Absolutely. I couldn't leave there soon enough."

Jill wagged a finger at him. "How dare you involve yourself with a Young Woman? You know her Rules."

They laughed. Previous to going off to Kenya, Jill's visits to Neal's digs had been viewed by his former landlady with a suspicion bordering on rudeness.

"You'll kindly leave your door open when that young woman calls, Mr Gallian."

Jill chattered herself to sleep as they drove back through the fading light of late afternoon, and it was dark when they reached Headington and drew up outside his flat. He gazed at her fondly before waking her, then shook her gently.

"Jill, we're here."

She awoke with a start, relaxing as her eyes met his. "Neal – where are we?"

"You'll see." He got out of the car, came round, opened the passenger door and helped her out. She looked confused, her gaze switching up and down the road, taking in the silhouettes of the estate's houses set against the starry sky.

"This is Headington," he said. "And my new accommodation. Remember?"

"Of course. You told me earlier."

She still seemed in a daze, so he took her by the hand, unlatched the front garden gate and led her down the path. Taking out a key, he unlocked the door and ushered her into a cramped hallway, flicking a switch to bathe it in light.

He indicated a door to his left. "The downstairs flat. Mr and Mrs Stone live there. They're both retired and very pleasant – you'll like them."

A flight of stairs stood to their right. Leading Jill by the hand, Neal climbed them, amused that so far for all her breathless chatter previously, she hadn't uttered a word since they'd walked inside. A quick glance showed that she was taking in her surroundings, her mouth hanging slightly open.

They reached the landing and another door, which he unlocked and pushed open. He switched on a light. "The upstairs flat," he announced, as he showed her in.

"But -?" she stammered. "Then, this is -?"

"Our flat. Where you'll be living when you're Mrs Gallian."

She let go his hand and wandered past him as if in a dream, walking the whole fourteen-foot length of the sitting room, taking in the scratched dining table and chairs, the G-Plan sofa (the room's sole new item), second-hand armchairs, the little Bush television set on its shelf, the ill-fitting curtains. She ducked into the bedroom, with its square of faded carpet left by the previous owner, the galley kitchen with newly installed refrigerator, bathroom with the plain white tiles which needed replacing or at least re-grouting. She returned to where he stood and beamed up at him.

"Oh, Neal, it – it's just – *fabulous*! I never expected – was sure we'd be living with Uncle Lam, at least to begin with…"

He took her in his arms, as she gazed up at him wonderingly. She was very young, barely twenty-three, whereas he was coming up for thirty-four. He was utterly floored by the sheer power of her love, her adoration, because he didn't feel there was much about him to be adored.

"Much as I like your uncle," he replied, "I think we need our own space, start as we mean to go on."

"I agree," she said, pulling away from him to survey the whole room. "Curtains," she went on, suddenly very businesslike. "I can make them. I'll measure up and get some material next week. And didn't I notice some paint tins in the bedroom?"

"I've been putting a coat on the window frames."

"I can help with that too, while you're at work. Just show me where you've got to. Oh, Neal, I really am so very happy. And you – well, you're just wonderful."

He smiled ruefully as he hugged her again. *Fabulous,* she'd said. He knew it wasn't that. It was a small, ordinary flat in an outlying part of the city, all he could afford. And wonderful – *him?*

He'd been for so long consumed by his demons, had desperately needed someone to chase them away. If anyone could, it'd be Jill, bringing a youthful freshness and zest to everything.

Neal recalled her pressing down on that towel less than eight months before, pressing with all her might and gratitude, as his blood soaked through it, staining her frock, hands and arms. *"Oh, Neal, my darling, please, please just hold on…"*

He'd held on, recovered from his second bullet wound, which had turned out to be nowhere near as serious as the first. And had found her waiting for him, fully committed to him in her devotion.

He made tea while Jill took several more twirls around the flat, gabbling excitedly away. They sat together on the newly acquired sofa to drink it, and Jill asked him to excuse her, she'd been in such a whirl and hadn't even asked about his work?

Neal replied that it was going well and on Monday he'd be tackling a new case. She knew something about the set-up, as she'd met most of his colleagues at the station's Christmas do: Don Pilling, Tom Wrightson – she'd especially liked Tom – Taff and Yvonne.

"I dare say you're going to be busy. But we'll agree on whatever I can do here, and I'll get on with it. Try and make my policeman's lot a happy one."

"Let's hope your policeman's wife will be happy too," he replied.

It was his major concern. There was as much pressure on the wife as on the husband, if not more. He'd never spoken to Jill about the abuse Helen Holt had suffered at her husband's hands, Clyde driven to distraction by the demands of the job and a failed promotion. There was more she'd need to know about both Clyde and Helen, but he couldn't bring himself to tell her yet.

He drew her into a clinch, wishing they were already married, wanting her so desperately. He decided they'd better not stay where they were for much longer.

Neal made a show of checking his watch. "We'd better get along to your uncle," he remarked. "He'll be worrying."

She smiled fondly. "Dear Uncle Lam. I'd almost forgotten him."

"He's organizing lunch for tomorrow."

The smile turned cynical. "Oh, yes?"

"But I'll be cooking it."

"Correction. *We'll* be cooking it. And I'm not letting you drive back to Oxford tonight. When I last wrote to him, I asked him to make sure he'd aired the bed in the spare room as well as mine."

Neal knew Colonel Wilkie didn't greatly approve of he and Jill staying in the same house overnight. But, as he pitched a few things into his duffel bag, he felt glad that he'd simply be around her – whether the colonel had remembered to air the bed or not.

*

Briar Hedge remained in the semi-muddle in which Neal had left it earlier. He noticed the vacuum cleaner standing forlornly in the corner it had occupied when Major Peaching had called that morning. He reckoned Peaching's visit would have rumbled along well into the afternoon with various accompaniments.

But it was a happy homecoming. Lambert Wilkie loved Jill as if she'd been his own daughter and was quite overcome at seeing her again. His own wife had died relatively young, and they'd had no children. Neal felt sorry for him, because he knew Jill's departure would leave a gaping hole in Wilkie's life, although they'd agreed for Jill to call in a couple of times a week, using Neal's old Ford Consul for the purpose, to cook, clean and garden for her uncle.

Neal would keep in regular touch too, because he got on well with Wilkie and they were both boosted by Jill's news that Ben and Janet Westmacott were planning to return to England on a permanent basis before long.

Fittingly, Sunday was a relaxing day. Neal and Jill went for a long walk through the woods and across fields to Braxbury and back after lunch, leaving Wilkie to his pipe. On their return, the colonel was dozing contentedly in his armchair.

Neal felt he should confide to Jill a few details concerning the case he was working on. She knew all about Clyde Holt's death and the gunman in the warehouse, whom Neal referred to as 'The Face'. He sensed her initial unease but assured her there was a long way to go, and any trail he followed might not necessarily lead to his quarry.

Before he left that evening, Neal handed Jill his spare set of keys to the flat. They'd agreed, for the sake of propriety, that she'd spend her nights at Briar Hedge, and he was determined not to rock any boats. Their leave-taking, in front of her uncle, was restrained, and Jill said she'd borrow Wilkie's Land Rover to drive to the flat in the morning, where she'd measure up for curtains and go to Cape's in St Ebbe's to choose and order the material. If Neal could get away, he'd drop by the flat for a bite of lunch in the middle of the day.

He drove back to Headington that evening, gently pushing thoughts of Jill to one side and reflecting on the seriousness of the case he was embarking upon, wondering where it might lead.

6

Neal arrived at the station early on Monday, as he wanted to catch DCI Pilling, whom he knew was likely to be out for most of the day on an inquiry. True to form, Pilling had his first pipe of the morning going nicely and listened intently as Neal updated him on what little he had to report so far.

Tom Wrightson had checked the records and found that the only theft of an Enfield revolver reported around the time of the break-in at the Ellisons' house had been, as he'd surmised, from the home of Major Peaching; indeed, it had been the only one in the whole of that calendar year. Still not conclusive, though, Tom had warned him.

Neal had spoken to Peaching at the weekend, although he'd learned nothing new. The gun had been stolen by Arnold Skelton, a local, small-time villain well known to the police, and Neal would use him as his starting point that morning.

Pilling nodded as he took this on board. "I can't underline this heavily enough, Neal," he said. "But the gun Skelton stole may not be the one we're after. I'm asking you to bear that in mind." His lips twitched in something approaching a grin. "But I doubt it'll stop you from following it up. See where it leads and keep me posted."

"Will do, Guv. I presume you're off out yourself this morning?"

"Yes. I've received a request from the Met. There's a counterfeiting gang from London distributing dodgy pound notes down here, and the Met have asked me to help from the Oxford angle. One of their chaps is coming down, and we'll be flushing out a few likely suspects."

"Well, best of luck."

"You, too. Oh, and don't forget Dakers is due to be with you at nine."

"I hadn't forgotten. Thanks, Guv."

He walked the few steps down the corridor to his own office when Tom Wrightson called out from the front desk. "Dakers'll be with you shortly, Neal."

Tom was grinning hugely, and Neal grinned back without knowing why as he entered his office. What was it about Dakers that the DCI and Tom found so amusing? Had the poor chap got two heads or a wooden leg? He supposed he'd find out before long.

Neal got behind his desk and worked away for a while at various reports concerning organized shoplifting in several of the city's big stores. He was concentrating on these when his door opened, and a polite female voice asked if he'd like a coffee.

"Yes, please." As he read on, he was vaguely aware of a woman setting down a cup and saucer on his desk and assumed she must be a new civilian member of staff. It made a change from grumpy Ethel from the canteen armed with her tea urn and moaning about the weather. "Oh, you'd better fetch one for the new DC, if you don't mind," he added. "I'm expecting him at any minute."

"Would that be Dakers?"

"Yes, that's right. How did you -?"

Neal looked up to find a tall young woman in blouse and pleated skirt, red hair twisted up into a bun, smiling down at him.

"WDC Sally Dakers reporting for duty, DS Gallian," she said brightly.

So that had been the reason for all their amusement. Dakers had been around the station for a few days, but the DCI and Tom had deliberately kept her identity from him, obviously intending that she'd be working with him. Typical police station humour, but Neal, as ever, took it in his stride. He guessed they'd known he would.

He returned her smile. "I'm only Acting DS, you know," he corrected mildly.

"And the only male colleague who hasn't looked affronted and said 'Oh, but you're a woman!'"

They both laughed, and Neal invited her to pull up a chair. She was certainly tall, not far off six feet he imagined, dwarfing the likes of Mal Brady, who just about scraped regulation height for a policeman.

Women in CID were still something of a rarity. There were a number of obstacles along the career path, and much of the fetching and carrying from the canteen, as well as other menial tasks, fell to the lot of the women detective constables, as well as the WPCs.

Neal asked Dakers about her background. She was from the north of the county and had spent some time as a WPC in Banbury before applying for a role in CID. After an initial training period, as Banbury already had a WDC, she'd been posted to Oxford and had found digs in Botley.

Dakers nodded towards Jill's photo, which stood in pride of place on Neal's desk. "She's pretty. Is she your wife?"

"My fiancée. We're getting married in the autumn."

"Oh, congratulations."

Neal's first impression was that he'd get along okay with Sally Dakers, but he wondered how she'd fare in the male preserve of Oxford nick. He guessed she'd find allies in the battle-hardened WPC contingent, particularly Yvonne Begley and Pam Harding, who often gave as good as they got; and that the DCI and Tom Wrightson would keep an eye on her, although they'd expect her to pull her weight. Taff Thomas and Mal Brady were a couple of lads, though, and he could imagine the new recruit being at their beck and call, particularly Brady's, if she didn't watch out.

He filled her in on their current inquiries, informing her of the situation so far regarding Derek Medway, and his own connection to the case concerning the Enfield revolver. "I'll be working that one," he confirmed.

"Mr Pilling mentioned the case," Sally Dakers replied. "He said about what happened to you, the -er, shooting. That must have been awful."

"It was," he agreed, deciding not to tell her that hadn't been the only time he'd stopped a bullet.

He went on to brief her about a series of corner shop hold-ups which had taken place in the first two months of 1962. One of the shopkeepers, Mr Brake, whose shop was in Rose Hill, had recognised the gun as an Enfield No. 2. Was it also the gun which had been used in the shootings? They needed to investigate, either to rule it out or establish a connection, and Neal wanted Dakers to re-interview the hold-up victims. Was there anything they could add to their original statements and, given that the incidents had happened over two years previously, might they have had any further thoughts which might help the police identify the gunman?

Neal installed her at Len Thackray's desk and handed her xeroxed copies, the paper shiny and blotched with smuts of toner, of the three shopkeepers' original statements. He outlined the shops' locations on a map of the city: Old Headington, Cowley Road and Rose Hill. It meant a lot of legwork but would help further familiarise her with different parts of the city.

Another long shot was to get her to show the hold-up victims an identikit picture of the Face, which Neal had helped put together when he was recovering from the warehouse shooting. Might someone recognise him?

Sally Dakers looked at it and shivered. "Wouldn't want to meet him on a dark night."

Me neither, Neal thought. *Although I did...*

He suggested she caught a bus from Queen Street up to Old Headington. There'd be more than enough walking to do after that. He ushered her out of the office and wished her the best of luck, as she went into the locker room to fetch her coat.

Tom Wrightson was at the desk, with Mal Brady in close proximity, looking rumpled in an overlong raincoat – his 'flasher mac', as Taff Thomas called it.

"You've met Dakers, then?" Tom called out with a wicked grin.

"Yes, Tom. And thanks. Remind me some time that I owe you and the DCI." But he was smiling as he said it, for there was never malice in any ribbing Tom dished out.

Sally Dakers walked past on her way out of the building moments later with a shy smile at them all, and Neal was aware of Brady monitoring her progress. He threw Neal a salacious grin. "Better mind how you go there, Gally. And you almost a married man."

"Ah, Mal," Neal threw back. "How good to see you. How are you faring with the job I gave you on Friday?"

Brady was immediately wary. "Oh, making progress."

"Good. So, how about making some more? Then we can have a chat about it this afternoon? I'll be back soon after three."

"Oh. Right. Yep – fine." Brady grinned feebly and sloped off in the direction of the canteen.

Tom Wrightson watched him go. "That's the way, Neal. You keep him at it. The DCI's been making noises about him slacking. Doesn't do a bad job once he's into it but often needs a kick up the backside to get him moving. You off out yourself now?"

"I'll be gone a while, Tom. Dakers has gone out to re-interview the corner shop hold-up victims and will report back later, if the DCI should ask."

"Very good, though I dare say he'll be out all day himself. Hope you get some sort of lead from this, Neal. Good luck."

Neal thanked him and left. It was what he was hoping too.

7

Neal didn't envy Sally Dakers her long walk across various parts of Oxford. His own journey was of a much shorter distance, as the Covered Market was little more than a quarter of a mile from the nick.

He entered at the bottom end in High Street, did so every time he passed through the Market. Nostalgia, he supposed, because he could never resist a peek in the windows of the pet shop, always recalling his six-year-old-self tugging on his mother's arm and begging her to buy a puppy he'd seen, a little black-and-white bundle of fur and fleas. She'd regretfully brushed aside his heartfelt plea. "Your father will never allow it, darling." And he knew she'd been right. Had she given in, Lionel Gallian would have made her drive back into Oxford and return it immediately.

Neal had always loved the Market: its plethora of butchers' shops, the invigorating tang of the fruit and vegetable stalls, the comfortable smell of leather goods. None of it had changed, and he walked briskly through to the Market Street end, his destination Colver's Fruit & Veg, a stall spanning the width of two aisles.

He picked out Arnie Skelton straight away from his unruly blond mop, servile in his brown overall as he attended to a customer, weighing up apples and potatoes and loading them into brown paper bags. Arnie's problem was that he always looked shifty, which was exactly what he was. Neal reckoned Major Peaching would have employed him because he'd come cheap, although with Arnie's type there'd always be a hidden agenda, which would usually reveal itself sooner rather than later.

As Neal approached, he caught sight of another figure, standing to the side of the stall. The man turned his back and walked away the moment he realised he'd been spotted. He was on the short side, probably late forties, flashy-smart in grey check overcoat, light blue flannels and Tyrolean hat. Neal delved into his memory bank for a name, found it quickly: Jerry Rudd, someone always in the know, often with information for which he'd expect to be paid; and it didn't always have to be the police who'd get the tip-off.

Where trust was concerned, Rudd was a long way down Neal's list, and he wondered why the man was hanging around Colver's stall. It was likely he'd been waiting to have a word with the gullible Skelton, in the hope of tapping into any useful knowledge he might have.

Neal stood a little way off while Skelton finished with his customer, going to the till and ringing up the purchase. He noticed Alf Colver keeping a watchful eye on the transaction, as Arnie placed a ten-shilling note in the till. Once he'd closed the drawer, Neal walked over to him.

"Morning, Arnie. Remember me?"

Skelton swivelled round, aghast. "Who the heck -? Oh." Recognition kicked in: Neal had felt his collar a few times in the past. "Yeah, right. Hey – didn't you quit the filth – er, beg pardon, the p'lice?"

"I did. But I'm back now, and I'd like a word."

Arnie dragged his gaze round to where Alf Colver stood looking on, shaking his head wearily. "What have you done now, Arnie?"

"Nothing, as far as I know," Neal answered for him. "Let's say it's a social call."

Alf's weathered face split in a slow grin. "Is it ever, with your lot? But don't keep him too long, will you? I'm short-handed today."

"He'll be back soon," Neal assured him. "Come on, Arnie." And he led the way across to Brown's Café, Arnie scurrying along beside him.

He bought them each coffee and a bun and carried the tray over to the least populated corner, switching a glance through the window in case Jerry Rudd happened to be lurking outside.

"So, what's this about, then?" Arnie inquired twitchily. "I remember your name now. Gallian, ain't it? You were one of the uniform boys."

"Plain clothes now," Neal informed him, "and looking into a case which goes back a while. Do you recall working for a Major Peaching out Islip way?"

Arnie plopped several sugar cubes into his coffee, picked up a spoon and stirred them. He hesitated, thinking. It looked painful. "Nah," he said at last. "Can't say I do."

Neal faced him squarely. "Think again, Arnie. It was just over two years ago, when you worked for him as a gardener and handyman, and your itchy fingers got you sent down for a stretch."

Arnie pretended to look enlightened. Again, painful. "Oh, right. I got him now. Ex-Army, weren't he? Decent enough sort but had the habit of leaving things lying around. Folk who do that, well, when they're that careless, it looks as if they want to give the stuff away, don't it?"

"It's one interpretation, I suppose," Neal conceded. "Even if it was the wrong one. After all, you got pinched."

Arnie Skelton shrugged ruefully. "Yeah, fair play. But I done my time for that. I got a good job with Mr Colver now, and I finished with that malarkey. I'm going straight."

There was a note of challenge in his voice. "Glad to hear it," Neal said, although he felt like inviting Arnie to pull the other one. He managed to keep his tongue in check. After all, he wanted information.

"Arnie, what interests me is the revolver you stole from Major Peaching. How quickly did you sell it on?"

Arnie frowned. "Sell it on? Dunno 'bout that, Mr Gallian. I *tried* to sell it to some geezers who didn't want it, left the pub, and they must've followed me, 'cause somebody fetched me a right wallop, and when I came to I was face down in the gutter, and the gun and cash I'd had on me were gone. You probably got it all in your files back at the nick. I told it all to some oldish bloke – plain clothes like yourself and not a bad bloke for a copper."

Len Thackray. Skelton was right. Len was a good bloke, and he'd clearly taken Arnie's story at face value, because they'd nabbed him bang to rights over the theft from Major Peaching, and he was going down for a stretch. In Len's eyes, it had been a result, and there'd been no need to push it any further.

But Neal, knowing that Peaching's revolver was their only available lead, wasn't prepared to accept it so readily.

"And now the true version, Arnie."

Skelton fidgeted in his seat and took refuge in his Chelsea bun, nibbling away at it nervously.

"Don't know what you mean, Mr Gallian. That was what happened, what I said at the time. Your bloke didn't see anything wrong with it."

"But you couldn't describe the men you met in the pub. You couldn't even be sure what pub you met them in."

"No, that's right. I said to your bloke, what with that blow on the head, I reckon I must've suffered loss of memory or summat."

Neal nodded as he took this on board and said nothing. Arnie Skelton continued nibbling at his bun, eyes fixed pleadingly on the detective's face.

"I don't believe you, Arnie," Neal said at last.

"But I've told you the truth…"

Neal was already shaking his head. "'Fraid your story doesn't wash with me. After all, you and the truth have always been distant relatives. I think you sold that gun on and couldn't own up to that, because you were scared the man you sold it to would come after you if you grassed on him."

Skelton's body seemed to sag, and his gaze dropped to his plate. He picked up his cup and took a couple of slurps of coffee to fortify himself but still wasn't able to look Neal in the face. Resistance had never been Arnie Skelton's forte.

Neal had gambled on the assumption that Arnie and his ilk were always economical with the truth, and there was a possibility that it was about to pay off. He fought to stay calm, wondering if, after two years, this might be the breakthrough. He pulled the Face's identikit picture from his jacket pocket, unfolded it and showed it to Arnie. It was a new xerox copy, but Neal hated the feel of it: tainted, cursed, as if it was smeared with his friend's blood.

"Was this the man?"

Skelton stared at it for a long moment. "Blimey – the face that sank a thousand ships."

"You've seen him before?"

Arnie shook his head. "Sorry, Mr Gallian. I don't recognise him."

Neal believed him. He took the sheet of paper back, folded it and returned it to his pocket. It would have been too easy. Besides, Don Pilling had had the whole station on the alert after the shootings. They'd interrogated everyone they could find. No-one had recognised the Face. And as for Skelton, he'd been inside at the time, halfway through a stretch of several months.

"Okay," Neal said. "I accept that. So, are you going to tell me who you sold it on to? I don't need to remind you, but it'd be best if you did."

Arnie swallowed. With an Adam's apple the size of a Cox's Orange Pippin, it was easy to see that he was on edge.

"Was it to Derek Medway?"

"Derek? Nah, Mr Gallian, not him. I knew Derek well. What would he want with a gun? I still can't believe he did that art geezer in. He just wasn't that sort. Hey, I seen in the *Mail* about what happened to him. D'you reckon someone popped him after the burglary so's he wouldn't get his share?"

It was an interesting theory. Neal made a mental note to get Mal Brady pushing harder to find out if one of Medway's known associates might have been the accomplice. The crooks and snouts tended to confide in Brady. With his rumpled raincoat, battered hat and down-at-heel shoes, they probably reckoned he was as dodgy as they were.

But Neal hadn't finished with Skelton, and the man flinched again under his scrutiny.

"The gun you stole, Arnie," he said sternly. "There's a chance it was used to kill Derek Medway."

He had no grounds for that hypothesis, but the effect on Skelton was startling. Derek Medway had been a mate, and they'd gone back a long way. Skelton looked devastated. "Swipe me, Mr Gallian. How – how was I to know?"

"You weren't. But it's my guess that when DS Thackray interviewed you, and you told him you'd been set upon and the gun taken from you, it was because you were too afraid to tell the truth."

Arnie Skelton looked up at last to meet Neal's penetrating stare. "Sorry, Mr Gallian," he gulped. "No, it wasn't the truth. I just got drunk and walked into a wall that night. That was the reason for the bruising and the crack on the head. Nobody took nothing from me."

Pilling had been right: they were into long shots, and this one had hit the mark. Neal was determined to go on trying them in his attempts to track down the gun.

Arnie spoke in a cowed voice which was almost a whisper, and Neal had to lean across the table to catch his words.

"I couldn't say nothing at the time. I mean, if I'd shopped him, he'd have killed me. It was Col Trevis, and you wouldn't have wanted to get the wrong side of him. He bought it off me. Said he wanted it for protection, 'cause someone was threatening his missus."

"And where do I find him?"

Something like a smirk wriggled across Skelton's face. "Cor, you have been out of circulation, haven't you? Col Trevis is well beyond the reach of your lot now."

Neal nodded, remembering. "Of course." And he knew where he could get full details on the late Mr Trevis: from Tom Wrightson, the station's very own Mr Memory.

He thanked Arnie for the information and made a note of his address, a room in a street behind the railway station. He got up, warning him not to leave Oxford without letting him know.

"Oh, by the way," Neal added, as Arnie was on the verge of escaping back to his market stall. "Why was Jerry Rudd sniffing around this morning? He made himself scarce when he saw me coming."

Arnie tried to look innocent, or as innocent as a serial sneak thief could manage. "He's always sniffing around, Mr Gallian. But he'll get nothing from me. My nose is clean, and it's staying that way."

"So I should hope," Neal replied.

Although I doubt it, he didn't add.

8

It was getting on in the afternoon, and Sally Dakers' feet were beginning to ache. Which, she supposed, served her right for having bought a new pair of shoes for starting this job. Still, much more walking and it wouldn't be long before she'd worn them in – or worn herself out.

Another problem was that this particular assignment was beginning to look like a waste of time. She'd visited two of the shops which had been robbed, but nothing new had come to light. The shopkeepers had both been rather vague, almost dismissive. "That all happened over two years ago. I'd more or less forgotten about it, and he actually got away with very little."

Sally had explained that she was calling because what had happened then might link into a current investigation, but all it got her were apologies and sympathetic smiles.

She stopped off at a little café for a sandwich and a cup of tea, desperate for something positive to report back to show she could be as much a part of the CID team as the men. Mr Pilling had warned her on her first day that, certainly to begin with, a lot of the more menial tasks would be likely to come her way, and that nice WPC, Yvonne, had told her to try to avoid being put upon by people like the genial Welshman, Taff, and particularly the scruffy little DC Brady. They were notorious, as she'd found when Brady pinched her bum squeezing his fat frame past her in the locker room earlier that day.

Sally thought she'd like working with DS Gallian, though. He was nice, good-looking too, and a bit different from the rest. She'd heard he'd been through a lot in the past couple of years. Before she'd met him for the first time that morning, Sergeant Wrightson had taken her aside and explained what had happened: how he'd got shot in the line of duty and his best friend and colleague killed, how he'd quit the force and none of them had thought he'd ever return. But Mr Pilling had wanted him back. There'd been something they'd both been involved in the previous year when Neal had been a civilian, and the DCI had been impressed by the way he'd handled himself. It was clear that the DCI and Sergeant Wrightson liked Neal very much (Tut, tut! She really mustn't think of him as Neal), and the girlfriend, Jill somebody, had helped persuade him to come back and give it another try.

She supposed he must be very much in love with this Jill. He kept her framed photograph on his desk, and he said they were getting married in the autumn. Still, she was very pretty, even if she did look as though she'd just left school. And it gave the lie to that daft phrase 'men don't make passes at girls who wear glasses.' More to the point, they didn't normally make them at tall, gawky redheads who were some way short of pretty – unless they happened to be sex-starved, scruffy, overweight policemen in a tumbledown Oxford nick.

*

Revived by two cups of tea and hoping she wouldn't need the loo, Sally trawled across East Oxford to Rose Hill. She knew she was in Rose Hill because she'd just passed its cemetery. A little farther on, she found Brake's General Stores, a neatly kept little corner shop with a smiling, curly-haired young woman in a flower-patterned housecoat standing behind the counter.

"I'm WDC Dakers, Oxford CID," Sally announced proudly. She was getting used to the introductory patter, finding that it rolled quite nicely off the tongue.

"Oh, hi. I'm Laura Brake. How can I help you, officer?"

Sally told her, adding that her inquiries were tied into an ongoing investigation and dreading a repeat of the answer she'd already heard twice that day.

But Laura Brake heard her out without interrupting. "Hhmm," she replied, frowning. "I remember I was out that evening, and Pa was in the shop on his own. Funny, y'know, but there was something he said the other day…"

"Is he here?" Sally asked, trying to subdue an unreasonable jolt of hope. She expected she was about to be told that he was out and wouldn't be back till late; or worse, that he'd gone on holiday.

"Oh yes, he's through in the back room, having a late lunch. I'll call him."

She leaned back and pushed open a door behind the counter. "Pa? Can you come through? There's a lady here from the police, and she's got something she wants to ask you."

"On my way," a distant voice called back, and the sound of scuffling footsteps gave way to the emergence of a short, grey-haired man in a dark blue overall. He smiled nervously on seeing Sally, and she introduced herself again and told him the purpose of her visit.

"Ah, good afternoon, miss. Harold Brake. You know, this is quite amazing. I only said to you the other day, didn't I, Laura? And I'll tell you, miss, it still keeps me awake at night, what happened in here more than two years ago. It's strange you should call in, because, oh, little more than a couple of weeks back…" He hesitated, looking doubtful. "Oh, but I'm sure it can't mean anything."

Laura rolled her eyes and sighed. "*Tell* the lady, Pa. Honestly, officer, he never stops telling *me*. For all we know, it may be of some help."

Sally Dakers was immediately on tenterhooks and likely to remain so for a while, as at that precise moment the shop bell pinged, and a customer walked in. Harold Brake smiled apologetically and sank down on to a stool behind the counter, while Laura attended to the customer.

She was a gossipy, middle-aged woman, who'd only called in for a small tin of baked beans, a Mother's Pride loaf and a quarter pound of liquorice comfits, but her visit stretched over ten long minutes, regaling the Brakes with the news of Mrs A expecting again – her fifth, and at her age! Mr B carrying on with that woman from the laundry, and young Miss C having picked up with a *most* unsuitable boy, and her parents church people and all.

Sally was wondering if the customer would ever leave, but Laura, the last word in patience, served her while smiling sweetly and making appropriate responses here and there, before escorting her to the door, opening it and ushering her out on to the street, still gossiping. Once she'd waved her off, she shut the door and put up the 'Closed' sign. "Just while Pa says his piece," she explained to Sally.

"The lad came in late one night," Harold began. "I say a lad, 'cause he talked like a youngish man. I couldn't see nothing of his face, 'cause he was wearing dark clothes and a balaclava – just his eyes showing. Well, he pulled this gun out of his coat pocket, and it's funny how you notice these things, ain't it? I saw right away it was an Enfield revolver, the sort I was issued with back in the war. He was waving it about as though he wasn't used to it, and, by crikey, I thought the blessed thing'd go off at any moment. Well, it had all happened so sudden that I came over a bit faint, sort of plonked down on this here stool. I'll give him his due: he seemed concerned, leaned over the counter and asked, "You alright, dad?" The faintness passed, I nodded and got up and he jerked the gun towards the till. I handed over the cash, and he left quickly."

Sally tried to look encouraging, despite experiencing a sinking feeling. What Harold Brake had just told her coincided almost word for word with the statement he'd made more than two years ago. But Harold hadn't finished.

"Couple of weeks back, this young lad came in one lunchtime. It was a perishing cold day, wasn't it, Laura, and he was muffled up in coat, hat and gloves with a scarf round his face. He wanted a packet of *Guards*, and they were up there on the top shelf. Well, I started to climb up and get 'em and missed my step on the darned ladder, ended up blundering into the shelves and falling to my knees.

"He stepped forward, kind of concerned. "You alright, dad?" he asked. I assured him I was, and he paid for his fags and left. But you see, miss, it was that same phrase and the way he said it. It struck me after he left that it sounded familiar, and I said to Laura that I wondered if it was the same bloke. Might be nothing in it at all, just the words and how they were spoken, well – they sounded as if they were spoken by the same man."

The same man? It was a straw, no more than that, and Sally Dakers snatched at it. She thought furiously and began piling on the questions.

Could either of the Brakes add anything to the man's description? Did he say anything else at all? Had he parked a vehicle outside the shop – a car, motorbike or push-bike? Was anyone waiting for him outside? Which way did he go when he left the shop?

Laura had been in the shop that lunchtime, stacking tins on the shelves. She shook her head. All she could remember was that he'd definitely been on foot.

"And you say this happened a couple of weeks ago?" Sally said. "Can you pinpoint the exact day?"

"Oh, let's have a think now," Harold replied. "About the end of the week, wasn't it, gal?"

"Yes, Pa. I'm sure it was a Friday."

"It was that." Harold reached up and snatched a calendar off its hook where it had hung down from the shelves. "Ah, here we are. Friday 6th March, miss."

Sally had pulled a notebook and pen from her handbag and was scribbling furiously away. She thanked the Brakes and asked them to ring the station and leave a message for her if they remembered anything else. "Anything at all. However small a detail, it could prove to be really important."

"So, you believe it might have been the same man on both occasions?" said Harold hopefully.

"It could well be," she replied.

She left the shop, eager to get back and report to DS Gallian. She didn't feel so weary now. Indeed, there was almost a spring in her step as she sought out the nearest bus stop for getting back down into town.

9

Neal hung around the Covered Market for a while. He made sure Arnie Skelton saw him walking away but once out of his line of vision doubled back and kept watch in case Jerry Rudd returned. Half-an-hour passed without a sight of him, and Neal decided to call it a morning.

He paid a quick visit to the flat. Jill was there, as she'd planned to be, measuring up for curtains. She'd borrowed her uncle's Land Rover to get to Headington and would use it to pop down to Cape's for curtain material before returning home to start work on it. Neal had time for a bite of lunch, cup of tea and a kiss before going back to the station, as he wanted to pick Tom Wrightson's brains before the sergeant went off shift. He promised Jill lunch in Oxford the next day, and they arranged that she'd meet him outside Crawford's in Queen Street at one o'clock.

He found Tom at his customary position behind the front desk.

"Colin Trevis, Tom," Neal asked. "What can you tell me about him?"

"By 'eck, lad," came the reply, "how long have you got?" Tom understood immediately that this was no casual inquiry and corralled PC Paul Hodgson who, for his sins, happened along at that moment, to take over at the desk while he and Neal discussed the matter in private.

Yvonne Begley had just dropped something off in Neal's office and, as it was mid-afternoon and she was likely to be heading for the canteen, Neal wondered if she'd mind fetching them each a cup of tea. He hated to ask, feeling that it placed him in the unenviable category of certain of his colleagues.

Yvonne's answer was a grin. "What I like about you, DS Gallian, is that you're always so polite."

Tom grinned back lopsidedly. "That's 'cause 'e were brung up proper, love – not like some of 'em."

He had been. Neal well remembered his father's encouraging hand on the few occasions he'd forgotten his manners.

"Colin Trevis was a villain through and through," Tom began, as they sat and drank their tea, accompanied by the digestive biscuits Yvonne had thoughtfully provided, "and he was a nasty piece of work to boot. Trouble was, we were never able to pin anything on him. And the only time we could was because someone stitched him up, and by then he was beyond being caught."

There'd been a couple of mail van robberies in the county during November '61, and Tom said he'd look out the file for Neal.

The robbers had done their homework regarding the mail van's route on each occasion. They'd prepared an ambush on a country road, using two stolen cars. The first car would tail the van, keeping a good distance between them. As the van approached a tight bend, the second car emerged from a gateway to block the road, forcing it to a sudden halt on the grass verge. Before the driver was able to reverse, the first car came up fast behind to prevent it.

The masked robber in the first car never got out. The other two, also masked, leapt out quickly, threatening the driver and guard with sawn-off shotguns. Blindfolded, and with their hands tied behind their backs, the hapless Royal Mail employees were bundled into a ditch, while the robbers transferred the mailbags to their cars and headed off. Each haul was reckoned to be worth upward of three thousand pounds.

It was so far, so good for the robbers, and they were persuaded to push their luck a step further. On Friday 15th December, an armoured van left a city centre bank with the accumulated wages of workers in local factories which included a Christmas bonus. It was thought the robbers must have been working with inside information, although the source was never traced. The roads through the city were busy with traffic, but there was one point where the van had to take a narrow approach road to reach its first port of call. It was here that the robbers had decided to stage their attempt.

However, the police had received an anonymous tip-off and were waiting for them. As before, the robbers' first car came out of nowhere and closed up behind the wages van. As he did so, the driver clocked a police car coming up fast behind him, and he panicked, screeching to a halt, leaping out and taking off on foot through a housing estate. He was never identified and never caught.

The second car had already burst out on to the road to head off the wages van. The driver saw the police car and took off in the opposite direction. Two hundred yards away, he came upon a police roadblock, two cars parked across the narrow road. For most villains it would have been enough, but the driver paid no heed. He was bent on escape, picking up speed and ploughing on to the grass verge to squeeze past the obstacles. Part of a low wall went with him, but he wasn't giving in, determined to reach the main road and the chance of freedom.

"The DCI was there," Tom said. "He was amazed when the car made it past without ending up in the wall. It might have been better for them if it had."

The fugitives made it to the by-pass, causing havoc at the Green Road roundabout. "Lucky no-one was killed," Tom added grimly. "Although disaster wasn't far away."

The robbers had a fast car, but the chasing police car was faster and its driver more skilful. It was closing up on them as they hit the A40 towards High Wycombe. In their haste to pull clear, they were overtaking on dangerous bends, took one far too fast and plummeted off the road, crashing into a wooded area.

"Roy Gorrie and Col Trevis," Tom said. "Both killed outright. Our boys managed to get the bodies clear before the petrol tank went up. In fact, Trevis was clear anyway, 'cause he'd been thrown through the windscreen. Gorrie would've got hold of the cars. He ran a dodgy garage out Horspath way, so had plenty of opportunity. We assumed Trevis had been the brains behind the robberies but had no way of proving that."

"And you never identified the bloke who did the runner?" Neal asked.

Tom shook his head. "Could've been anyone. We asked around Trevis' and Gorrie's known associates but drew a blank. One or two we fancied, but they'd got themselves solid alibis."

"And the tip-off? Any ideas?"

"I took the call out front here. A woman, voice deliberately muffled. No-one I recognised." Tom took his last mouthful of biscuit, chewed it ruminatively. "So, lad – why all the interest in Col Trevis? He's long gone."

"Because it turns out that Arnie Skelton sold him that Enfield revolver he'd nicked from Major Peaching. Trevis reckoned someone was threatening his missus, and he wanted it for protection." Neal grinned as Tom pulled a face. "I don't buy that either," he went on. "And yet it doesn't appear that the revolver was used in the mail van robberies?"

"No, Neal. Trevis and Gorrie used a couple of sawn-offs. Scared those poor Royal Mail lads out of their wits. Still, who would have fancied being on the end of a blast from one of them? As for Trevis wanting the revolver for protection, he certainly wanted it for something, but it wouldn't have been that. Don't know if you knew Col, but he was a big bloke, ex-boxer and really intimidating. Anyone 'ud have thought twice before taking him on. My guess is that Col sold the gun to someone. He'd have browbeaten little Arnie into letting him have it for a knockdown price, then moved it on at a decent profit. Great one for wheeling and dealing was our Col. His proper job was as a self-employed painter and decorator, but we always guessed it was a cover for shadier goings-on. Trouble was, we could never prove it.

"One thing I can tell you, that revolver wasn't at Col's house. We turned the place over, Taff and me. Not a sniff of anything incriminating. Gloria – his missus – pretended she knew nothing about her husband's activities. But take it from me, she knew alright. By the by, Neal, it'd be worth having a word with the lovely Gloria. The address is in the file, and she's still there.

"Col was a ladies' man, you see, and I reckon the tip-off about the wages van might have come from some floozie he'd thrown over. Might even have been Gloria herself, 'cause by all accounts, things weren't good between her and Col, and it was reckoned she might have been playing the field herself. I'll leave it in your capable hands, lad."

Neal thanked Tom for the information and went along with him to Records to look out the files on Colin Trevis and the mail van robberies. He returned to his office with an armful of folders and noticed Mal Brady talking to Paul Hodgson at the desk.

"Ah, there you are, Mal," he greeted him. "Come on in. Good day?" He closed the door behind them and indicated the seat which Tom Wrightson had lately vacated. Mal pitched down on to it, wearing his usual hard-done-by expression.

"Same old story, Gally," he said. "And the usual guff about Derek Medway, how he was a crook through and through but there was never anything violent or aggressive about him. Everybody I spoke to was shocked that he'd ended up the way he did.

"I -er, dropped into the Carpenters Arms lunchtime," Brady went on matter-of-factly. (*I'll bet you did,* Neal thought). "I know Doris, you see, Derek's mum, as well as some of her customers. Couple of old lags there – one of 'em was Dick Jolley. Remember him? He was a mate of Derek's dad and had known Derek since he was a nipper, but I'd say he'd not got it in him to be anybody's accomplice, and as for the others," Mal reeled off a couple of names, "they wouldn't know one end of a revolver from the other. And of course, as far as Arnie Skelton was concerned, he was in custody at the time."

Neal thanked Mal for the work he'd done, even though they could both could have predicted the end result. He asked him to keep a look-out for anyone who might have been associated with Colin Trevis.

"Trevis?" Mal frowned. "He's been gone a couple of years, Gally."

"I know. And Arnie sold him the revolver which I believe did for Medway. I'm keen to track it down, so see what you can come up with. Also, keep an eye open for Jerry Rudd. I'd like a word with him."

"Reckon he's involved in this, then?"

"He could be involved in anything. I clocked him in the Covered Market this morning, hovering round Arnie Skelton. I'm sure he's up to something."

"Always is and always has been," Mal sighed.

Neal sent Brady off to refresh himself with a cup of tea in the canteen, although he was certain Mal would already have had ample refreshment during the day. If only he could be as assiduous in his other duties.

Neal settled down to study the contents of his folders, until a knock sounded at the door and WDC Sally Dakers walked in full of the joys of spring.

10

Neal was in the DCI's office early the following morning to update him on progress and wondering if what they'd achieved thus far merited that description. He spoke about Harold Brake's recent visit from the man he felt might have carried out the hold-up in his shop two years previously. Neal currently had Dakers working on possible reasons for the man calling in. Did he actually live nearby? Had he been visiting someone? Was he perhaps a company rep passing through the area at intervals?

Pilling was already shaking his head. He didn't seem in the best of moods, and this wasn't going to improve it. "All very thin, Sergeant." He'd sat slumped in his chair but now straightened up a little, as if not wanting to sound too discouraging. "Dakers, Neal. Early days, I know, but what do you reckon to her? It looks like we have to get used to women detectives in CID. My old guvnor 'ud go up the wall at the very idea."

"She strikes me as competent, Guv. She's not scared of work and seems out to prove she's as good as any of the other DCs."

"Not a lot of competition where Brady's concerned," the DCI grumbled. "You're keeping him busy I trust?"

"He's chasing up friends and associates of Colin Trevis."

"Col Trevis?" Pilling perked up, immediately interested. "He's long departed and darned good riddance too. So, where does he fit in?"

"We got a lead on that stolen revolver, Guv. Arnie Skelton sold it on to Trevis."

Pilling frowned. "Trevis was involved in those mail van robberies and got himself killed when he and his crew tried to ambush that wages van."

"Tom's already given me chapter and verse on those."

The DCI's mouth twitched in almost a grin. "Nothing to add there, then. But as I recall, Trevis and his mate used shotguns. We never came across a revolver."

"Precisely. So, why did he need it? Skelton told me Col wanted it because someone was threatening his wife, but I'm not giving that the time of day."

"Me neither. And of course, Neal, the revolver Skelton stole may not be the one you're after. You need to bear that in mind."

Another reminder, as if he needed it. "I'm fully aware of that, Guv. But this is the only lead we've got, and I need to follow it through."

Pilling's gaze was fully on his DS, registering his determination. "Keep me posted, that's all."

"Will do, Guv." Neal got up and walked to the door. "Any result from yesterday?" he asked, feeling it diplomatic to do so but sensing from his boss's mood that the operation hadn't been a rip-roaring success.

The DCI shrugged. "We've certainly made some progress and managed to put the finger on one or two operators. But, as I might have suspected, they're small fry and the big fish is nice and secure, directing operations from behind, no doubt, a mask of respectability. The Met have got their work cut out with this one."

Neal commiserated with his boss, knowing the last thing he'd want would be sympathy, and returned to his office where Sally Dakers was just finishing a phone call.

"Thanks for calling. That's really very helpful. 'Bye."

She replaced the receiver in its cradle and turned towards him, her face aglow.

"I take it that's good news?" he ventured needlessly.

"It's something, Sarge." Sally's voice was charged with enthusiasm. "That was Laura Brake from the Rose Hill corner shop. When that young man called in on 6th March, she recalled there must have been traces of mud on his shoes. Soon after he'd left, she noticed a smear of mud on the mat in the doorway. She's sure it had to have been left by him."

"How was he dressed?"

"Quite smartly. Dark overcoat, black brogues. It was a cold morning, and his face was muffled in a scarf."

"Obviously he hadn't walked across a ploughed field, then. Right, I've got a call to make. You sit here and give it some thought. There's a city map in the top drawer of your desk. While I'm gone, you can try to work out where our man might have been, in or near Rose Hill, to have got mud on his shoes." He nodded at the pile of paperwork he'd left on her desk. "You can think about it while you're filing that lot away."

*

The little terraced houses in the skein of narrow streets halfway up the Cowley Road were squeezed tightly together as if to stave off the chill of the March morning. Neal parked the Anglia and walked round to a house in the next street.

Gloria Trevis answered his knock at the door. She was in her thirties, a dolled-up peroxide blonde in a bulging blouse, tight blue skirt and black calf-length boots. He'd learned from Tom Wrightson that, even though she had a job, she might be supplementing her income through other activities. Neal didn't have to wonder what these might be, as he was alert to a door closing softly at the top of the stairs.

Gloria's manner was less than welcoming. "What d'you want?"

Neal produced his warrant card. "Police, Mrs Trevis."

"Blow me, I'd never have guessed. Make it quick, will you? I'm on my way to work."

"Where might that be?"

"The supermarket down near the Plain if you must know. I work in the office. Why? What's it to you?"

"Can I come in?"

"If you must."

Neal cast a glance over his shoulder. Two women were gossiping in a doorway across the road, and he guessed he must be the object of their interest.

"Probably best if I do."

Gloria stood aside to let him in, fixing the gossips with a basilisk stare before slamming the door. She pushed past him into the downstairs room, flung herself down on the faux-leather sofa and snatched up a pack of cigarettes and a lighter off the coffee table. She lit up and stared at him defiantly, pointedly neglecting to invite him to sit.

"Why this visit, then?" There was aggression in every line of her face, and she dragged heavily on the cigarette, sending an unwelcome plume of smoke in his direction.

"I'm trying to trace a gun," Neal replied levelly.

"Well, you won't find one here."

"It was sold to your late husband."

"He's not here either, thank God."

"The gun's possibly linked to a murder which took place several weeks before Colin died. He told the man he bought it from that it was for protection, because someone was threatening you."

"Ha!" Gloria threw back her head and laughed cynically. "As if he ever cared! And besides, *he* was the only person who ever threatened me – and often did more than blimmin' threaten!"

"You should have reported him to us, Mrs Trevis. We could have done something about that."

Gloria shrugged carelessly. "I'd have been down at the nick every day without fail. Anyway, I'd never have felt safe if I'd crossed Col. He'd have killed me; I'm not kidding you. Beat me black and blue enough times, if I said so much as a word out of place. I couldn't have put up with that or his carryings-on much longer." She blew out some more smoke, not in his direction this time. It amounted almost to a peace offering. "Listen, copper. I never knew about any gun, and that's God's truth. That business with all them robberies, well, you could've knocked me down with a feather when I heard he'd been behind them. Your lot were crawling all over the house after Col got killed, and they found nothing. If he had a gun, he must've sold it on. 'Cause whatever he was involved in, he never left a sniff of it here."

Neal tried another tack. "What do you know about the people he mixed with, Mrs Trevis?"

Gloria grimaced. "I kept out of their way as much as I could. Roy Gorrie was round here a lot. He was a slob, and I couldn't stand him, with his lewd suggestions if Col didn't happen to be around. Sometimes, when I was out with Col, we might run into people like Arnie Skelton, that slimy little toad Rudd, and then kids whose names I never knew and wouldn't care to. People hung around Col, 'cause he was always buying and selling dodgy goods. Not that there was any need, 'cause he was doing okay with his business – painter and decorator – and he was no slouch at that. Earned good money doing up a lot of them posh houses in North Oxford, Cumnor and the like. But he couldn't ever have left it there. Going straight was never enough for him."

"You said something earlier about his carryings-on. What did you mean by that?"

Gloria Trevis looked fierce again, dashing out the remains of her cigarette in the ashtray on the table. "What d'you think? Women. Another of Col's problems was that he thought he was God's gift. He had a thing going with that singer down at the Blue Dahlia in St Clements. Didn't realise I knew all about it. Loretta Taine – and that's not her real name either. Apparently, she's still there – got to be as old as the hills. And of course, whenever any of his lady loves gave him the heave-ho, yours truly was right here, on hand as a nice, convenient punchbag."

"So, I take it things are better now?" Neal asked.

She smiled for the first time, briefly and reluctantly. He guessed she'd probably been pretty once, but it would have been a while ago. "Yeah. S'pose you could say that."

He thanked her, and she followed him to the door. As he pulled it open, he heard the slight creak of a bedspring from upstairs. "Got a visitor?" he asked mildly.

The smile became a snarl. "Mind your own bleedin' business." She reached out and snatched a red PVC mac from a hook at the foot of the stairs. "You can buzz off now. I got to get to work."

Neal left, pausing to watch as Gloria slammed the door and flounced off down the street. He went round the corner, keeping the house in view in case someone emerged. When, after a while, no-one did, he got into the car and drove back to the station.

11

Detective Constable Mal Brady always carried out a quick reconnaissance of the front desk area and corridor before entering the building, because he never knew who might be around. The DCI was always after him for something or other, and Tom Wrightson came a close second. They'd scarcely give a bloke time to draw breath before sending him here, there and everywhere to carry out their instructions. Now he was getting earache from *Acting* DS Neal Gallian too, and beginning to wish Gallian hadn't allowed himself to be persuaded to re-join the force.

But today the coast was clear. It looked like Uncle Tom was on the late shift because PC Taff Thomas was manning the desk. Uncle was showing him the ropes to prepare Taff for when he sat his sergeants' exam. Onward and flippin' upward. Mal shook his head wearily: just what was *wrong* with these people?

He stopped by and passed the time of day with Taff, interrupting his concentration on his paperwork as he leaned imperiously on the desk and began stirring the pot, as he usually did. He nodded in the direction of Neal's closed office door.

"Gally closeted in there with the ginger Amazon, then, Taff? Hhmm. Needs to watch his step, doesn't he, 'cause I doubt that nice little gal of his'll be too pleased?"

"Stop knocking him, Malky," Taff scolded in his cosy Welsh lilt. "Gally's not there. He was off out early on inquiries. Dakers is working in there alone."

Brady grinned salaciously. "Oh, right? Don't reckon I'd leave her in there alone."

Taff rolled his eyes. "Oh? Fancy her, do you?"

"Well, she's a woman."

Taff looked taken aback. "Blimey, Malky, you don't say! No wonder you're working in CID. Have to say, though, I prefer 'em not quite so tall myself." He glanced down at Mal from his six-foot-plus vantage point. "Bit tall for you too, I'd have said."

"Ah, go and boil your head, you big Welsh git," Mal threw back. "And what are you going to do once you get those stripes? Reckon you'll get rid of Uncle Tom so easily? Take it from me, *boyo,* when he goes, they'll have to carry him out feet first."

"Once I've got the stripes, I'll have to go where there's an opening," Taff answered comfortably. "And who knows where that'll be? But one thing I do know, Malky boy, I'll have had 'em a long while before you get to make it to DS."

"DCI's ruddy blue-eyed boy got in there before me, didn't he?" Brady grumbled. "Jammy devil's got everything going for him."

"Don't begrudge him a bit of luck now," Taff chided. "The lad's been to hell and back. He deserves a break." But Mal wasn't listening.

Sally Dakers had just emerged from Neal's office, and Brady greeted her with a leer.

"Ah, Dakers. Make yourself useful, will you, love? Pop up to the Market and get me a couple of cheese and pickle sandwiches – much better than those curled-up things they serve in the canteen. Any time now'll do nicely. Haven't had a bite to eat since breakfast."

Unknown to Brady, Acting DS Gallian had just come through the door and had heard every word. Taff Thomas saw him and grinned.

"How about you fetching them yourself, Mal?" Neal was gratified to see Brady whirl round, startled, and Thomas's grin widened, as he pretended to be absorbed in his paperwork. "After all, the exercise'll do you good."

Dakers remained in the office doorway, looking uncertain but inwardly glad that someone had come to her rescue. She'd only been at the station a few days, and already Brady was becoming a pest.

"Your services don't seem to be required, WDC Dakers," Neal went on easily. "DC Brady's decided he has to watch his figure. You cut along to the canteen and have yourself a quick break. Mal and I need to use the office."

Dakers smiled, relieved. "Thanks, Sarge." She turned and walked off down the corridor, while Neal ushered a sullen-looking Brady into his office and pointed him to a seat.

"Go a bit easy on her, Mal," he said reasonably. "We all indulge in a bit of banter 'cause we're used to it, but Dakers is new to the job and needs the chance to find her feet."

"Okay, Gally," Brady sighed. "Message received and understood." He realised there was no point in making an issue of it, and he was happy to climb down – for now.

"So, how's it going?" Neal asked, when they were both seated.

"Drawing a blank, really," Mal grumbled. "Trevis is history, Gally, a forgotten man. Most people I spoke to were frightened of him and not too upset that he's gone. I leaned on Skelton a bit, but of course, when Medway burgled that art place, Skelton was in custody. He knows nothing. Jerry Rudd's in the know about most things, but I've not been able to pin him down. Medway and Skelton followed Trevis around and did whatever he asked of them. Hey, though, I've been thinking…" Neal had guessed that had been the case from Mal's tortured expression. "What would you reckon to Col being Medway's accomplice – although I'd say he'd be more the controlling presence? 'Cause if Medway didn't come up with the goods – and apparently there hadn't been a lot of money in that safe – it would have been just like Col to have turned nasty."

"It's a decent theory, Mal," Neal agreed, although somehow it didn't feel as simple as that to him. It could well have been that Trevis had shot Medway – in fact, it was looking likely – but what had happened to the gun after that? To whom had Trevis sold it or passed it on?

"Better keep digging, then, Mal," he went on. "And here's another little task for you: find out who Gloria Trevis is seeing these days. There may well be a link back to Col."

"I'll see what I can do," Brady replied. "I'd say she's bound sure to be seeing someone. I'll get on to it now."

Well, more or less now, he was thinking, deciding he'd give the canteen a miss and grab a hot meal in the Covered Market. It'd give him valuable thinking time without some *Acting* Detective Sergeant looming at his shoulder.

*

Sally Dakers picked up a cup of tea and a KitKat in the canteen and made her way over to where the two WPCs Yvonne and Pam were sitting and having a natter, well away from the table where several of their male colleagues were involved in an argument as to whether it would be Liverpool or Manchester United who'd win the First Division championship that season.

She was about to ask the ladies if she could join them, but they beat her to it, pulling out a chair and smiling a welcome. Sally still felt very new and guessed she would for some time yet, but Yvonne Begley and Pam Harding, both a few years older than her, had been very kind and welcoming from the start.

"You look a bit frazzled, dear," Pam greeted her, as Sally sat down beside them. "Don't tell me that irritating little squirt Brady has been bothering you?"

"He keeps pestering me to run errands for him," Sally sighed.

"Well, just say no," Yvonne advised her. "It's not as if he outranks you. There's enough running about to do for Mr Pilling and Sergeant Wrightson – but they happen to be the ones in charge."

"And you have to look on that as all part of the job," Pam added. "At least you're working with Acting DS Gallian. He's different altogether – always so polite. We were really glad when he returned to the force, and Mr Pilling was adamant that he'd be working back here. It's early days, I know, but what's he like to work with?"

Sally suspected she was blushing slightly, but the two smiling WPCs pretended not to notice. "Yes, he's, well – different. I like him."

"We all do," said Yvonne. "And after all, Sally, we're the ones who count. Things wouldn't get done without us around." She sighed. "I don't think DS Thackray will be coming back, poor man. The doctor's told him he has to have complete rest, and he's not that far off retirement anyway."

"No, and Mr Pilling's always liked Neal." Pam tittered girlishly. "Sorry, we always refer to him as Neal between ourselves but mustn't let Sergeant Wrightson catch us doing it."

Sally smiled. At least she wasn't alone.

"I dare say if DS Thackray doesn't return," Pam went on, "Mr Pilling will want Neal to replace him. He's so brave, coming back after all that's happened. You know about that, do you?"

"Yes," Sally replied. "Mr Pilling told me. It must have been awful."

"I'm sure it was," Yvonne said. "But it turned out well. He's back here, and he's engaged to a really nice girl. He deserves some luck." She glanced at her watch. "Hey, look at the time. Pam, we'd better get our skates on. I'm due on the city centre beat with one of the new PCs."

"And I'm heading for that school in Marston," Pam gasped. "Better speak nicely to PC Hodgson and see if he'll give me a lift up there. Lovely to chat with you, Sally. We must do it again."

"And often," Yvonne added, as she pushed back her chair. "Chin up, Sally. And don't stand for any nonsense."

12

Taff Thomas looked up to see Dakers glancing warily around as she returned from the canteen. "Mal's hooked off, love," he greeted her with a wide grin. "He'll be out of your hair for a while." He followed up his observation with a wink.

Oh Lord, not another one, Sally thought. It wasn't as if she was remotely close to resembling Brigitte Bardot or Claudia Cardinale. She was long and thin, and her classmates had called her 'Carrot Tops' at school. She smiled back weakly and headed for the safety of the office.

DS Gallian looked up as she hesitated in the doorway. "Come in and take a seat, Dakers," he invited. "Did you get anything?" He directed a nod towards the desk where the pile of paperwork had lain. "By the way, well done with that lot."

"Oh, right. Thanks, Sarge."

"All that filing didn't interrupt the thought processes, then?"

"Oh – no. Well, I have been giving it a lot of thought. You see, I believe Friday 6th was a wet day. What if the man who called into the shop had been to a funeral? Rose Hill cemetery's nearby. He was in smart clothes, and the mud on his shoe might have come from the graveside."

The DS considered this for a moment. "Sounds plausible. There's your next job, then. Check back on any burials that might have taken place there that day."

"I already have, Sarge. A Miss Wayfleet, who lived locally. Her burial took place that morning." Sally pulled a notebook from her skirt pocket. "Eleven-thirty, and the undertakers were Dorran and Crane from Littlemore. Their contact was the lady's niece, a Mrs Jevons, who lives in Headington."

DS Gallian puffed out his cheeks and grinned widely. "Don't hang around waiting for something to happen, do you, Dakers? That's excellent work."

Sally beamed back, a little flushed and overwhelmed by the compliment. But she sensed a keenness about him and, more than that, a little tension. Perhaps he felt they might be a tad closer to the man he was seeking, the one he called the Face. But surely Neal was realistic enough to know that it was still speculation? The gun the young man had had when he'd held up Mr Brake might not be *the* gun, and Sally wondered how deflated he'd be if it turned out that it wasn't.

But he was quickly businesslike again. He set her the task of contacting Mrs Jevons through the undertakers, visiting her and finding out from her the names of the people who'd been at the graveside. She'd also need to obtain their addresses.

"I hope you won't need to visit all of them," he went on. "And I'm afraid you're going to have to tell a white lie. You'd better say to Mrs Jevons that there was a minor incident in Rose Hill – a handbag snatch – at around the time of her aunt's burial, and you're looking for anyone who might have witnessed it as they came away from the cemetery. As discreetly as you can, find out the names of any youngish men who attended – they'll probably be relatives of the dead woman. But tread carefully, Dakers. We can't afford to make anyone suspicious, and the last thing we want is to frighten anyone off."

Sally nodded her understanding, got up and lifted her coat off the peg behind the door. Taff Thomas looked up as she appeared in the corridor. "Dakers, tell DS Gallian he's got a visitor," he called out.

But Neal had already heard and had followed her out.

A girl was standing by the desk, fair hair brushing her shoulders, slim and smart in a brown suede coat, pleated skirt and low-heeled pumps.

"Jill!"

He dashed past Sally, almost running up to the desk, Taff looking on with a wistful smile.

The girl was laughing, and Sally had to admit she really was very pretty.

"Don't tell me you'd forgotten we were meeting for lunch, Neal Gallian?" she teased him.

"I hadn't forgotten, honestly. Didn't we say Crawford's Cafeteria, at one o'clock?"

"We did. And I got into town a bit early, so thought I'd come down and meet you."

"And you won't find me quarrelling with that. Oh!" He turned, suddenly alert to Sally standing behind him. "You know Taff, but you won't have met our new recruit. This is WDC Dakers."

The girl was already stretching out a hand and smiling a welcome. "Jill Westmacott."

"Sally Dakers. Pleased to meet you." They shook hands, Sally having to admit that Jill wasn't only pretty but seemed a very nice person too. And registering the ecstatic gleam in Neal's eyes told her she'd have to put that particular daydream firmly back on the shelf.

"I'll be on my way, then, Sarge," she said.

"Fine, Dakers. Best of luck."

As Sally left the station on her way to the bus stop, she looked round and saw them walking hand in hand along the opposite pavement. It was quite obvious that Neal adored her, and Jill must feel so safe and snug with her strong, handsome man to protect her. Someone had said she'd been a teacher. Huh! She looked as if she was only just out of school herself.

Sally gave herself a mental slap on the wrist. "What's your problem, Dakers?" she muttered under her breath. "Are you jealous or something?"

The answer followed on immediately. *"You bet!"*

*

"Had a productive morning?" Neal asked, as he and Jill sat opposite one another in the cafeteria, having placed their order.

"Making progress," Jill replied. "You'll see when you get back tonight. The new curtains are up in the sitting room, and I'll work on the bedroom ones at home. The pair I took down are unlined, but I can hang them over the window on the landing."

"Wow! You've been busy."

She smiled. "I shouldn't think you've been exactly idle yourself."

"No, things are ticking along. How's the colonel?"

"Banished to the summerhouse during daylight hours, so that I can clean through the house properly. He tells me he's away tomorrow night at another of his reunions. He let me borrow the Land Rover today, but I'll have to come in by bus for the next two."

"You can have my car. I've put you on the insurance."

Jill shook her head. "I don't mind the bus. I've just picked up the most recent Agatha Christie from the library. I really need to catch up on my reading."

Their meals were brought to the table, and they ate in silence for a while.

Neal had been aware of Jill casting him little up-from-under glances. It was because she knew full well what he was going to say.

"I don't like the idea of you staying alone at Briar Hedge."

She reached across and covered his hand with hers. "Darling, how many times have I stayed in that house on my own? Uncle Lam's often away at some do or other, and I don't want him to feel he shouldn't be getting out and about. I'm just glad he keeps in touch with his old friends and colleagues."

"Yes, you *used* to stay there alone. But that was before I knew you."

"Neal, we have got neighbours in the lane, and every house has a telephone."

"And the nearest house is at least a hundred yards away. Listen, why don't you stay at the flat?"

"I met Mr and Mrs Stone from downstairs for the first time this morning. They're really nice. But we're not married yet, and they could easily get the wrong impression."

"Are you saying my intentions aren't honourable?" He pretended to be hurt.

"I know they are, you poor old thing. But *they* don't."

"Well, all I can say, darling, is that it's a pity."

She gave his hand a squeeze. "And all I can say is that I agree. And that September's not far away."

"Suppose not."

Jill was looking directly at him, and he saw that unmistakeable gleam of love in her eyes. They clasped hands and smiled warmly at one another. He vowed then in his heart, as if he hadn't done so before, that he would do and be his best for her, try to deserve her devotion.

They finished their meals, passed on dessert and lingered over coffee. Silence set in again, and Neal sensed she was working up to a question.

"Neal, I've been wondering."

"What about, darling?"

"You. This case. Listen, I don't want you fretting too much over it. I know you want to track down this man who killed your friend, but – well – life's more important: our life together."

He sat and marvelled at her. She was very young but seemed to possess a wisdom beyond her years. She'd picked up on the tension about him, something he'd deny to anyone but her, if challenged.

It was just a feeling he had, that he was beginning to close in. But was he? *It may not even be the gun.* He recalled the DCI's words of warning; the occasional look of concern Tom Wrightson had thrown him. He needed to take a step back if he could. The last thing he wanted was to betray the trust they'd shown in him.

Neal paid for their meals and gave Jill a lift back to the flat. He suggested he drive her back to Briar Hedge the next two nights, but she refused. "You may not be free," she argued. "Mr Pilling's offering you this promotion on a plate, it seems to me, and you've got to be committed. Your job comes first."

"It never will," he replied. "You come first – and don't forget it."

As he drove back to the station, Neal realised that he was properly in love for the first time, and that it was a wonderful feeling, stronger than ever in the few days since Jill had returned from Kenya.

And because of that, he guessed he'd worry about her even more.

13

Yet Neal found himself in an unexpectedly pliant mood when he arrived back at the station, feeling much calmer for having taken that lunch break with Jill. She had, of course, been right: the tension, expectation, had started to get to him, and he made a mental note there and then never to neglect her, no matter how pressing the demands of the job.

He settled himself in his office, certain that Dakers wouldn't be back for quite a while and knowing that Brady was out somewhere, making sure he steered clear of Neal. He'd have to insist on a daily update on progress where his somewhat recalcitrant colleague was concerned.

There was more paperwork to get through, logging the results of his visit to Gloria Trevis, as well as the issue he had Dakers looking into, and he worked away for a good hour before he was distracted by the far from dulcet tones of Tom Wrightson barking into the phone at the front desk.

"Yes, sir. I understand. But you're not to approach him, do you hear me? It's highly likely he's dangerous. He may even be armed. I'm sending a team of officers out to you now. They'll be with you in about twenty minutes. And I repeat – don't approach him!"

He slammed down the receiver as Neal, disturbed by the commotion, appeared in the office doorway. "Taff!" Tom yelled. "Fetch Hodgson from the Records office! Mardon Farm, out towards Tackley, double quick! Ah, Neal, we're going to need another driver. The DCI -."

But the DCI was already charging down the corridor, in the act of jamming his hat on his head.

"Mardon Farm near Tackley, sir," Tom repeated. "Farmer discovered him fast asleep in a barn, if you ever did."

"Let's nab him before he can make a break for it," Pilling suggested. "Come on, DS Gallian. Time to show me you can still drive a police car. Tom, get Thomas and Hodgson to follow on behind. They'll know where they're heading. Right, Sergeant, let's go."

As they roared up the Woodstock Road in the police Zephyr with its siren blaring and the sound of Taff's siren not far behind, Pilling explained the reason for the high state of excitement.

A convict, Henry Alton, serving a long stretch for rape and assault, had escaped from Grantonwood Prison near Bicester a few hours previously. Members of the public had been advised not to approach him. The news had broken that lunchtime, and the farmer at Mardon Farm, out towards Tackley, had just informed Tom that there was a man asleep in his barn. He was dressed in an overcoat and hat which the farmer was sure he'd last seen on a scarecrow in one of his fields, probably in an attempt to conceal his prison garb.

As they drove, Neal revelled in this unexpected opportunity to be at the wheel again, having fully engaged with his time on the squad cars and several high-speed chases in which he'd participated. Once they were beyond the confines of the city, Pilling advised him to switch off the siren and patched through to Taff's car to tell him to do the same. They were still some miles off Mardon Farm, but the noise would carry, and he didn't want to give their quarry an early warning of their approach.

Neal slowed as they turned into the lane which led to the farm. A little way down it, a round, tousle-haired man in dungarees and wellingtons spotted them and started gesticulating feverishly up the lane. Neal brought the car to a halt alongside him, and he and the DCI climbed out, just as Taff and Paul Hodgson drew up behind them.

"I heard about it on the lunchtime news," the farmer gabbled excitedly. "It's him, I'm sure of it. I came out of the barn and, blow me, there he was, fast asleep on some hay bales."

"We'll take it from here, then, sir." Pilling's voice rang with authority. "I'm DCI Pilling, Oxford CID, and this is DS Gallian. You are?"

"Joe Melrose. I own the farm."

"Right, Mr Melrose. You wait here, please. This man may be dangerous. Is there a back entrance to the barn?"

"Yes, there is, and it's my guess he came in that way."

Pilling nodded brusquely. "Thomas, Hodgson, get round to the back of the barn and wait for my signal. But stay well back – behind that far hedge, for instance. Gallian, there'll be a megaphone in the boot of our car. Pass it out to me, please."

Taff and Hodgson set off, while Neal fetched the megaphone and handed it to his boss. Pilling turned back to the farmer. "We'll approach the barn from the front. You stay the far side of the cars, sir. Gallian, we'll wait for our chaps to get into position."

"Yes, Guv."

Minutes later, responding to Taff's distant wave, they began walking slowly across the farmyard. The ominous bulge in the DCI's coat pocket told Neal that his boss was taking no chances. It took him back to the warehouse, when he and Clyde Holt had been unarmed, to the deadly blast of the Face's gun, Clyde on the floor and himself catapulted back, falling, clutching his shoulder…

That same shoulder tweaked uncomfortably, a grim reminder, as he and Pilling took cover behind a tractor parked in front of the barn. Deep inside it, they could make out the figure of a man in ragged clothes stretched across a couple of hay bales, dead to the world.

Pilling raised the megaphone. "This is the police. You are surrounded. Come out of there slowly with your hands up."

His voice boomed out across the Oxfordshire countryside, having a startling effect on the man, now sleeping, now jerked unceremoniously into unwilling life. He leapt to his feet, looked wildly about him, fell over across a bale and staggered upright again. He was unkempt and unshaven, dressed in a tatty overcoat and battered hat. Finally seeming to realise his dilemma, he blundered away towards the rear of the barn, where he hauled open a door.

"I seem to recognise him," Neal whispered.

"Hhmm." The DCI's expression was grim. "You're right. He looks familiar – and well known to us." As the man disappeared from their view, Pilling bawled into the megaphone again. "Thomas! Hodgson! He's heading your way! He's *not* armed. Repeat, *not* armed."

"And not dangerous either," he sighed, lowering the megaphone. "What a ruddy waste of time. Come on, Sergeant, let's do what we've got to do."

They emerged from their cover and waited for the two constables to bring the fugitive round to the front of the barn. They'd handcuffed his wrists behind his back, and Hodgson was trying to steer him in something like a straight line while holding him at arm's length.

"Billy Maggs, sir," Taff Thomas reported, as they approached.

"Thought I recognised him," Pilling grunted.

"Sir, he stinks to high heaven and he's as drunk as a lord," Paul Hodgson complained.

"So, what do you want me to do, Hodgson? Treat him to a wash and brush-up and mix him some Andrews' liver salts? Take him back to the nick and book him for being drunk and disorderly." Pilling wafted away an unhealthy odour from under his nose. "Then hose him down, bin those God-forsaken rags and look out some clothes from lost property. Farmer reckons he could have borrowed them from a scarecrow."

"He did, sir," Taff piped up. "There's a naked scarecrow in the next field."

"Theft as well, then," Pilling added gruffly, although his lips were threatening a grin. "And once he's safely in a cell, smelling less offensive, get yourselves a strong cup of tea and a breath of fresh air. In fact, several breaths."

The two constables nodded, grinned stoically and escorted the stumbling Maggs to their car. Once they'd driven off, the DCI called over the farmer and asked him to accompany them into the barn.

"He wasn't our escaped convict, Mr Melrose," he explained. "Although he's well known to us. Thank you for spotting him and alerting us so quickly. Let's have a dekko in the barn, just to see if our Billy's caused any damage. Oh, and apparently there's a denuded scarecrow in one of your fields, so you were right about the clothes."

They checked through the barn, finding a couple of empty beer bottles and one which, by its pungent smell, had contained meths. No damage had been done, and Melrose, relieved that he hadn't been entertaining a dangerous escaped convict, remarked that he'd look out some more clothes to spare the scarecrow's blushes.

"So, what now, Guv?" Neal asked, as he turned the car round in the farmyard and set off at a more sedate speed than that at which they'd arrived. "Back to the nick?"

"Er, no." Pilling glanced at his watch. For once, he was looking uncertain, even a little embarrassed. "Would you drop me outside the cinema on the Cowley Road, Neal? I'd intended finishing early this afternoon because I've arranged to meet my wife there. It'll be getting on for six o'clock by the time we get back."

"Never had you down as a film fan, Guv?"

"No, well, I'm not. It's just that Sheila's been nagging me for weeks to see this film, and I've finally given in."

"Oh, right. What's the film?"

"The -er, *Pink Panther* or something. Have you seen it? There's some detective in it, and she reckons he reminds her of me."

Neal had to work hard to withhold a smile, privately complimenting the long-suffering Sheila Pilling on her sense of humour. "Ah, yes. I saw it earlier in the year. It's very good."

"This detective, then? Is he some sort of super sleuth?"

"Something along those lines, Guv. Whether you'll identify with any of his methods, I don't know. But I'm sure you'll enjoy the film."

14

After a while, Neal had had enough of paperwork. However, before he headed for home, there was a call he needed to make.

The Blue Dahlia nightclub was situated in a side street off St Clements, its presence announced by a blue neon sign and entrance gained up a narrow flight of steps. It was early evening, and the bar hadn't long opened, with a few customers perched on its stools and several lounging on the maroon Dralon seating which lined its walls.

"I'm looking for Loretta Taine."

The chubby barman, bald head already glistening beneath the spotlights over the bar, stared wearily at Neal's warrant card. "You'll find her downstairs, mate," he murmured flatly. "Dare say you'll hear her warbling before you see her. But don't pull her in just yet – the customers might not be happy." He grinned tightly. "Doubt if the boss will either."

"Not that sort of visit," Neal grinned back. But he could hear her already as he turned away from the bar, a seductive, smoky voice promising *Our Day Will Come,* which he recalled had been only a minor hit in Britain the previous year, despite having hit top spot in the USA.

Another, much wider flight of steps led down on to a carpeted area, riddled with small, round tables, each with two chairs, the wall lighting artfully dim, creating an intimate venue for men not bringing their wives. Across the parqueted dance floor, there was seating for a small orchestra and beside it a grand piano, at which a smiling accompanist, false dark hair gleaming with brilliantine, accompanied the singer.

Loretta Taine stood beside the piano, one hand resting upon it, rehearsing the number before an otherwise empty room. She was glamorous, glossy pink lips and green eye shadow, her blonde hair curving down below her jawline. A long, glittering evening dress was cut low to advertise generous breasts. At first glance, Neal put her somewhere in her early thirties but on drawing closer he got the distinct impression that she'd not see forty again.

Taking a seat at one of the tables, he parked his hat on it and waited for the song to end. Once it had, the accompanist closed the piano lid, nodded curtly in Neal's direction and disappeared through a door at the back of the room, while Loretta Taine snatched up a pack of cigarettes and a lighter from the table beside her and walked forward with a welcoming smile and practised sway to where Neal sat.

"I take it you're looking for me, love?"

"If you're Loretta Taine?" He stood and pulled out a chair for her.

"Sounds better than Gladys Marble, wouldn't you say?"

Neal smiled. "By some distance. I'm Acting DS Neal Gallian, Oxford CID."

Loretta fluttered unmissable eyelashes at him as she sat down. "Oh dear, what have I done now?"

"Nothing, as far as I know."

"Not going to arrest me, then?" she pouted, pulling a cigarette from the pack and lighting up. It was some French brand, which looked expensive. He guessed she was, too.

"Probably not today."

"Oh. Pity." Her gaze swept over him appraisingly. "But you're bound to be spoken for anyway. Tell her from me that she's a lucky girl." She took a long drag on her cigarette, blew a ring of smoke at the high ceiling. "So, how can I help, love?"

"It's a murder inquiry," Neal informed her. "It happened a while ago. You remember Colin Trevis?"

"Col?" Her painted eyes were suddenly wary. "Sure, I remember him. He was a difficult guy to forget."

Neal supposed he would have been for any woman who'd been involved with him. He recalled a photograph in the file he'd been reading about the van robberies: a fair-haired, muscular-looking man with an insolent smile.

"You were -er, friendly with him?"

Loretta Taine laughed unmusically. "We were what you might call bosom pals. Col was an irresistible kind of bloke, and it was a pity it ended the way it did. We had a good thing going."

"You must have had some idea of what he was up to, then? The mail vans, the wages snatch which went wrong?"

Loretta was eyeing him cagily from behind a cloud of smoke. "Me, love? No, I was completely in the dark about his other activities. You could've knocked me down with a feather when it all came out. No, Col kept all that sort of thing very much to himself, which is how he managed to steer clear of your lot for so long. He'd always had something on the go, and most of his deals would be dodgy. Don't understand why he couldn't have gone straight, 'cause he earned good money with the painting and decorating. Never quite enough for him, I suppose. He always liked to have plenty of money to splash around, plenty of excitement in his life."

"This is where you first met him, at the Blue Dahlia?"

"Sure. He was often in here, usually up in the bar area with his mates. One night, he came down here to see the show, we got talking and drinking, and one thing led to another."

"And these deals he was involved in? They took place here?"

She shrugged. "It gets busy up in the bar, you get all sorts there. It's a good place for money to change hands."

"I'm trying to track down some of the people he hung around with. Anyone you know?"

"Well, let's put it this way: *they* tended to hang around him. Quite a few young lads looked up to him, as well as some not so young. That bloke who was in the paper the other day, the one that got buried in a field. Med-something?"

"Derek Medway. It's his murder we're investigating."

"Arnie Skelton was in here a lot. That man Rudd – he's really creepy - always gives me the shivers. And there was a cousin of Col's used to trail round everywhere after him. Very young lad, Micky something. Otherwise, kids who came and went, friends of this Micky. A lot of money changed hands, and Col's were the hands it usually ended up in."

"Money changing hands, eh?" Neal kept his tone light. "What for? Drugs?"

Loretta looked affronted, and Neal wondered if she'd ever tried her hand at acting. "Drugs? Not here, love. Never known 'em here. We just wouldn't allow that sort of thing, or our licence 'ud go up in smoke."

Neal nodded compliantly. He needed to keep her on-side and wondered how she'd react to his next question.

"The wages van snatch that went wrong. We were tipped off about that by an anonymous phone call – a woman's voice…"

She was already shaking her head, staring back at him coolly. "You need say no more." There was steel in her voice: he'd guessed she'd have a hard edge. He'd rattled her with his not-quite-an-accusation, but there was no way she'd lose her rag: she'd always keep the upper hand.

Loretta confined her anger to stabbing out the last of her cigarette in the ashtray on the table. "If you reckon that's the sort of thing I'd do, you can think again. Listen, love, Col told me he'd quarrelled with his cow of a wife. He was sick and tired of the way she was putting it about, and he was on the verge of walking out on her and moving in with me. Maybe you should be looking in her direction. A woman scorned, and all that. I'm sure you can work it out."

Neal already had where Loretta Taine was concerned and wasn't prepared to labour the point. He took the familiar xeroxed sheet from his jacket pocket, by now hating the rumpled, soiled feel of it.

"The lads who hung around Col Trevis," he said. "Might this have been one of them?"

Loretta studied the picture with a moue of distaste. "It might have been. I can't say for sure. Listen, love, I was only ever vaguely aware of these lads. They hung around in the bar, and I might have said hi to some of them in passing, but I rarely went in there." She chuckled throatily. "The gentlemen usually insist on serving the drinks to me. Anyway, doubt if I'd have looked twice at this bloke. He's scary."

There was something else, Neal thought, as he glanced at the picture before folding and returning it to his pocket. The Face looked hunted – which was exactly what he was. Surely someone would recognise him, and soon? Although, he reasoned, no-one had recognised him in the investigation after the shooting. So, why should they now? He could be anywhere in the world.

Loretta had started to fidget. Neal had been aware of movement and the hum of voices behind him. He guessed the bar was filling up and realised that a couple of the tables close by were already occupied. He guessed Loretta would be 'on' before long, and business beginning in earnest.

"One last thing," he said. "Who owns this place?"

"Sam Diamond," she replied with a pert grin. "Has done since it started up after the war. I was still in school those days in case you're wondering. Sam takes more of a back seat now. Sunning himself in the Caribbean at the moment, lucky beggar. This is a straight business, love. Take it from me, there's nothing dodgy about it."

He grinned back, amused. That was good, coming from someone who'd been more than close to Col Trevis. Neal picked up his hat, thanked her and left. She was a cool one, and he guessed she'd have been more than a match for Col if he'd ever started to get heavy with her.

15

Loretta Taine's remark about the young men who'd hung around Trevis had given Neal an idea. He called at the bar on his way through, caught the barman at a slack moment and showed him the Face's picture.

The barman gave it a long look and shook his head. "Hundreds of blokes pass through here, mate. I don't recognise him, and he's got the sort of ugly mug that'd stay in the memory. Sorry."

As Neal thanked him and turned away, he heard his name called, the voice close to a conspiratorial whisper. He looked round and spied Mal Brady at a table tucked into a corner behind the bar. He went over, directing a curt nod at the pint glass in Brady's fist.

"Drinking on duty, Mal? Good job I'm not the DCI."

"Unpaid overtime, Gally." Brady's tone was carefree. "A mark of my dedication to the job. So, what brings you down here? Apart from queering my pitch?"

"Following a line of inquiry," Neal replied, wondering how many 'pitches' Brady might have in and around Oxford, and how many of them might serve alcohol.

His colleague grinned impudently. "Same as me, then. You wanted Jerry Rudd tracked down. Well, he's here – straight across from the bar, with a group of blokes. Looks like they're having a friendly game of cards."

Neal pulled out a chair and looked in the direction Brady had indicated. It was Jerry Rudd alright, flashily dapper in an offensive heather mixture suit, thinning blond-grey hair stretched back across his skull and looking every inch the conman he was, as he conversed with the three young men around him, who were attentive to his every word.

"Finish your drink, Mal," Neal said, "and wait out the front to intercept him. Now we've got him, I definitely want a word. The minute I wander over in his direction, he'll clock me and make himself scarce. Oh, and good work, by the way."

"Doubt if you'll get much out of him for free," Brady warned.

"I doubt that too," came the reply.

Brady finished his drink, stifled a belch, got up and ambled away. Neal gave him a minute to get outside, then rose and strolled, as if aimlessly, over to where Rudd and his friends were sitting.

At a mumbled warning from one of the men, Rudd looked up and clocked Neal's approach. A spasm of alarm passed across his face. "I'm out, fellas. Got to see a man about a dog." Neal noticed the pack of playing cards he slipped deftly into a jacket pocket.

Rudd pushed back his chair and scurried away, jamming his Tyrolean hat on his head and giving Neal a wide berth. Neal nodded at the group of men, one of whom smiled wanly while the rest studiously avoided eye contact. He walked briskly past them in the direction his quarry had gone.

Outside, Mal Brady had Rudd trapped at the foot of the steps, and the little conman swivelled round as he heard Neal's footsteps descending towards him. He grinned nervously. "What's this all about, then? Hey, you're that copper I saw in the market yes'day, ain't you?"

"Acting DS Gallian. I saw you too, Jerry. You were hassling Arnie Skelton." He directed a nod towards Mal. "You'll know DC Brady, of course."

Despite the chilly evening, there was a line of perspiration above Rudd's upper lip.

"No, you got me wrong, officer. I wasn't hassling Arnie, cross my heart. Me and him go back a long way. Old friends we are."

"Well, we don't need to talk about that right now. There's something else I want to ask you. Let's go back inside. It's a bit warmer in there."

"Er, no." Rudd shook his head emphatically. "Best not. Er, p'raps just have a chat round the corner here?"

"Okay." Obviously, Jerry didn't want his potential customers to see him hobnobbing with the law. Neal led the way along the street and turned into the mouth of an alley, with Rudd behind him and Brady bringing up the rear.

Once they were out of sight and the street beyond them empty, Jerry Rudd recaptured some of his customary swagger. Neal was sure he'd been entertaining – another word for fleecing – three gullible companions with 'Find the Lady' or some other card trick. Whatever, there was always going to be something in it for Jerry.

"What is it you want to know, then, officer?" His tone was outwardly polite and helpful, but Neal didn't have to look too far to discover the usual insolence beneath.

"I need some information."

"Oh, right. I'm good at providing that."

"I don't doubt it. It's an old case that we're trying to clear up. You remember Colin Trevis? He used to get down to the Dahlia a lot."

"Right. You bet he did. Seeing that sexy singer, wasn't he? Wish I was."

Neal pursed his lips as he wondered how flattered or otherwise Loretta Taine might be if she heard that. Probably otherwise.

"We know Trevis did a lot of deals down here. This would have been not long before he died, late November or early December of '61. He sold someone a revolver, and I want to find out who bought it. You must have some idea who used to get down here around then?"

Jerry Rudd considered this for a moment. "Mostly young lads, all impressionable. Col 'ud get 'em paying over the odds, making 'em believe they'd got a good deal. Hhmm, difficult to recall any names…" He left the sentence hanging in the air.

"You're sure?"

There was a crafty glint in Jerry Rudd's eye. "Well – if I think hard enough, I might come up with one."

"Not Arnie Skelton?"

"Nah. Stupid berk had already got himself nicked, hadn't he?"

"Who, then?" Neal dug a hand in his trouser pocket and brought out a one-pound note, which Rudd eyed with contempt.

"Stroll on! I thought you were serious about this?"

Neal replaced it with a fiver, and Rudd, mean eyes gleaming, shot out a hand, but Neal had already closed his fist on the note. "A name first, Jerry," he said.

Rudd looked sullen for a moment, contemplating holding out before giving in with a shrug. "Micky Parkin."

"Col's cousin?"

"Yep. He was always trailing round after Col. Rumour has it, he was shafting Col's missus – bit of an age gap there. Col wouldn't have been pleased if he'd heard about that. No sirree, he wouldn't have been pleased at all."

And for a consideration, you wouldn't have let on to him, Neal was thinking. He said, "So where do I find Micky Parkin?"

"He works nights up at Pressed Steel. Other times, no need to look further than the lovely Gloria's."

"Okay, I'll get to see him. But listen, Jerry. I don't want Parkin warned off. Is that understood? If he gets wind of this, we might decide to take a closer look at you."

Rudd was looking pale. "Yep. Message received and understood." He took the note Neal held out to him with something short of enthusiasm.

"And if you come up with any more relevant information," Neal added, "I'd be happy to make you some -er, small consideration."

Rudd nodded and bolted off down the street, his evening at the Blue Dahlia curtailed probably much sooner and less profitably than he'd intended.

Neal nodded at Brady. "Well done for tracking him down, Mal. The DCI'll get to know of this."

"Cheers, Gally. I'll be on my way now. See you in the morning."

"Sure."

He watched Mal go and prepared to move on himself but was distracted by the sound of a car drawing up behind him. Looking round, he saw a Cortina not ten yards away and thought he should recognise it.

As he pondered this, the driver's door swung open and Dale Corlett stepped out, smooth in a trendy blue check suit. There was a definite spring in his step as he hurried up into the club.

Intrigued, Neal followed him, making sure to keep a reasonable distance between them. He arrived in time to see Corlett cross the dance floor and pull open the door beyond the piano. He neglected to close it properly behind him and, moving closer, Neal had a glimpse of a corridor with doors on either side. Corlett knocked discreetly on one of these, and it was answered immediately by Loretta Taine, who promptly enveloped him in her waiting arms, before drawing him into the room and closing the door.

Neal didn't wait around, having seen enough to get a handle on the situation. He chuckled softly. In his opinion, the ultra-smooth Corlett was playing a very dangerous game, because Loretta and Nadine Ellison were two formidable women, and he could imagine their reaction if they ever found out what was going on.

On top of that, he had to wonder what connection, other than Loretta Taine, Dale Corlett might have with the Blue Dahlia.

16

Neal parked the Anglia in the yard at the side of the station, locked it and went in to deposit the keys at the front desk. Paul Hodgson looked up from his paperwork as Neal came in.

"Someone's been looking for you, Gally," he remarked. "A lady, not a quarter of an hour ago. I said I thought you'd be back before long."

"She leave a name?" Neal asked.

"No, but she said she'd be in touch."

Neal was intrigued. It couldn't have been Jill, because she was known to most of his colleagues, including Hodgson. So, might it be something to do with the case?

Neal thanked him, left the keys in the office and, wishing Hodgson goodnight, walked out to where he'd parked his Consul that morning in a corner of the yard. As he drew closer, he caught a movement beside it and heard the scrape of a woman's heels before a figure emerged out of the shadow and into the yard's pale light.

Recognising her, he stopped in his tracks, and she approached him diffidently.

"Hello, Neal. It's been a long time."

"Helen."

She walked up to him, her smile as uncertain as her greeting. "How are you?"

"I'm fine. And you?"

"Fine." She extended a hand, a jerky movement, as if she was doubtful of a welcome, but he reached out and shook it briefly.

The station's side door opened and clanged shut, and someone, seeing them, called out a cheerful "Goodnight!" Neal returned the greeting, not sure who it was, but from the voice and his glimpse of a uniform beneath a light-coloured mac, he was persuaded that it must be either Yvonne or Pam, neither of whom would be likely to linger and eavesdrop on a private conversation.

If, indeed, that was what it was.

"The young constable at the desk said I was welcome to wait inside," Helen Holt explained. "But I couldn't. There were too many memories."

"I understand."

She switched him a glance, making proper eye contact for the first time. "Not only of Clyde," she added softly.

He answered with a nod, trying to be dismissive. He didn't want to go there, not at this or any other time.

"It'd be good to catch up," she persisted. "Is there somewhere we could talk – away from here?"

The best bet at that time of night would be a pub. There were several up towards Carfax, but any of his colleagues might be there, enjoying a quick drink or two on the way home after their shift. He had a vision of Mal Brady, the station's worst gossip by a mile, who might be in any pub in Oxford during opening hours. It was fortunate that it had been Paul Hodgson at the desk because he wouldn't have known Helen Holt. Neither Uncle Tom nor Taff would have pried, but both would have wondered and looked their question, and Neal's face would have provided an answer.

"Sure," he said. "Let's head down over the bridge. I know a quiet pub there." He was sure Brady's meandering route home wouldn't have taken him in that direction.

She smiled gratefully. Perhaps it was all she wanted: to catch up. But why? She'd been the one who'd walked away, who hadn't returned his letters, the one he hadn't heard from in almost two years.

As he'd hoped, the small pub down beyond Folly Bridge was quiet: just themselves and one elderly couple in the snug. Neal ordered a half of mild for himself and a lemonade shandy for Helen, taking them back to the corner table where she was seated.

It was the first proper glimpse he'd had of her. Her dark hair was shorter than previously and lightly permed. She was smartly but not expensively dressed in a light grey overcoat, grey skirt and black court shoes. She'd not gone overboard on the make-up, hadn't needed to, for she'd always had a healthy complexion, in the days when it wasn't punctuated by bruises.

Helen thanked him for the drink as he set it down. He sat across the small table from her, and she leaned confidentially towards him, although no-one was likely to be listening in.

"Neal, this has been on my mind a long time, and finally I decided I had to come and apologise to you. That time you were in hospital, my behaviour towards you was awful, and I'm sorry. Please – can you forgive me?"

He'd been shocked by her anger, paralysed by the savage indictments issuing from those same lips which had previously smiled upon him with such easy invitation. He recalled those ensuing weeks of misery, floundering in a pit of deep despair.

Things were different now. He'd been borne out of that cloying darkness into the light of a new and promising day. His answer was spontaneous, coming from the heart.

"Of course. I did some time ago. Because you were upset at the time – you'd only just lost your husband. And your words hit home. You were right: I could and should have saved him. I reacted too slowly."

"You did your best. I understand that now and should have done so then. And you came close to getting killed yourself. I hope the shoulder's healed?"

"It gives me a reminder now and then. But I got off lightly. Clyde didn't."

They fell silent, as if remembering. He'd returned to the force, thanks to Uncle Tom's encouragement, Don Pilling's refusal to take no for an answer. Part of the reason had been because there was a duty still to be done, but he couldn't share that with Helen.

"I -er, heard you'd gone up to Scotland to stay with your sister," he ventured at last.

"Yes, for a while." Her gaze sought and found his. He felt he recognised a plea there. "Until I got back on my feet – or came to my senses. I moved back down this way. It's where I was brought up and where I belong."

"Back to Oxford?"

"Not far away. Northampton. My mum's sister lives there, and we've always been close. She gave me a roof over my head, and I do some secretarial work to help pay my way." She hesitated for a moment. "This is my first time back in Oxford."

"Visiting friends?"

"Just visiting."

He could tell she was summoning up courage to say what she'd come to say, and it was proving difficult. She'd been a bright, confident girl, but the years had taken their toll, dulling the brightness, eroding the confidence.

"I came particularly to see you," she went on at last. "The wounds – mine – are healing. And I realise I made a mistake."

"In leaving Oxford?"

"In that, and in hurting you."

"You said it just now, Helen. The wounds are healing – mine too."

"I'm glad."

Her hand reached across the table and covered his. He didn't react, felt, strangely, almost cold towards her. Had the wounds healed? At that precise moment, he couldn't be sure.

Slowly, she withdrew her hand, as if sensing his antipathy. "I – I just came to say sorry." There was a catch in her voice, a hint of petulance.

He sought to chase it away with a smile. "That's all in the past."

She tried a new tack. "You're still living in Headington?"

"Not at the old flat," he replied. "After all that happened, I couldn't face staying there any longer. I moved into digs for a while, but I'm back in another part of Headington now." He sensed her gaze on his face, sensed a tension between them. "I'm getting married in September."

"Oh – congratulations." She was smiling bravely. "That's really good news. I needn't ask if she's a nice girl because she's bound to be. And no more than you deserve, after all that's happened."

"And what about you?"

Her response sounded as if it had been rehearsed. He wondered if she'd been waiting to learn how things stood with him before she shared her news.

"At something of a crossroads, really. I'm friendly with an older man. His wife's terminally ill, and you know how people talk. She's nearing the end now, and I thought it diplomatic to withdraw for a while. Perhaps later – although whether he'll need me then, I don't know."

It was the Helen he remembered who'd been speaking: the old Helen – quiet, compassionate and caring. "It's a pity, Neal, isn't it? And I blame myself, not you."

She'd come round at last, but far too late. Neal wondered if they might have married if she'd stayed around, or if the affair would have simply blown out? Clyde's death had decided it for them.

"Arthur's a gentleman in every way," Helen was continuing wistfully. "Like you. I don't know how much longer I could have stayed with Clyde. His moods, bitterness and the violence – all that took something out of me."

"The job changed him," Neal reflected grimly. "Those months he spent working in CID. They brought about the change, although no-one's ever mentioned anything."

"Something happened. I asked him more than once, but he wouldn't say. And things just got worse between us." She smiled, and he saw the sadness in it, the regret. But not for Clyde. For them.

Helen started to get to her feet. "It's time I was getting back."

"To Northampton?" He doubted there'd be a coach, as it was well after nine o'clock.

"I'm staying in a guest house up the Banbury Road. I'll be going home tomorrow."

He couldn't answer that, hoped the relief wasn't showing on his face. "Time I was going too," he said.

They walked back up the road to the next bus stop. Neal felt awkward. His Consul was in the station yard, and he felt he should offer her a lift. There'd be comings and goings at the nick, and they were bound to run into someone. But the offer had to be made.

"No, Neal." Helen's tone was resolute. "I'll just hop on a bus. There's a stop right outside the place I'm staying, so I've no distance to walk. You get on home. I dare say you've had a long day. And I'm really glad you came back to the force. Clyde always said you'd climb higher."

He withheld a smile, recalling that Clyde had never said as much to him. Or was it just Helen, a reminder of her generous heart of old?

He waited beside her until a bus came along. She turned towards him as it drew into the stop.

"It's been good to meet up again, Neal. All the best for the future."

"You too, Helen."

They each moved a step closer, shared a brief, ungainly hug, then drew apart. Her sad smile reflected his own. Neal watched as she boarded the bus and found a seat. He returned her wave, watched as the bus drove her away into the night. It was a relief to see her go.

He made his way back to the station to pick up his car. He felt sorry for her, though. *"At something of a crossroads,"* she'd said, and he could well believe it. But she'd walked out of his life when he'd hoped fervently that she might stay and had left him wounded, broken and confused.

It had been Jill who'd picked him up, revived and renewed him. And he desperately needed to move out of the long shadow cast by those old sins.

If he could.

17

As he settled down in the woodland shack, shivering in the chill of the evening, and the steady rain slithered insidiously through the trees and dripped through several holes in the roof, Henry Alton reflected on the sheer cleverness of his escape that morning. And wondered if it had been so clever after all.

He'd begun the day working in the prison yard, shovelling coal. It was the job he hated above all others, and the screw who'd put him on to it was aware of that. Well, Alton decided he was going to do something about it and quick.

"Ooohh!"

He flung down his shovel and clutched his back, writhing in agony. It was a masterful performance, which he'd bear in mind for future use: the stomach next time, perhaps.

"What the heck's the matter with you, Alton?" snapped the overseer, as he stalked over towards him.

"Flamin' back spasms," Alton gasped. "I told Mr Morris I've been suffering from 'em, but he still put me on this blasted job."

"Only because he likes you so much," the man chuckled nastily. "Go on, hobble off to the sick bay and get the doc to check you out. He'll probably tell you to toughen up and get back here at the double, you weak-kneed, little toe-rag."

"You wouldn't call me that if you had to put up with this pain," Alton groaned. "You've no idea how I'm suffering."

"Oh, bring on the violins, why don't you? Go on, Alton, do me a favour and get out of my sight."

The doctor was a doddery old fool who ought to have been pensioned off years before, but Alton knew how to play up to him, ramp up the agonised expression and get a couple of days in the infirmary. It had worked before. He was oohing and aahing like a good 'un as he staggered into the doc's surgery, even if the miserable screw who was on guard duty in the waiting room looked far from convinced.

"Let's take a look at you," the doc said wearily, as he closed the door and invited Alton to strip down to the waist.

He'd just done so when there came a fearful hammering on the door, and the screw barged in. "Doc! You'd better come quick! Bloke just collapsed out here!"

"Oh, my goodness!" The doctor dithered for a moment, then, excusing himself to Alton, snatched up his bag and hurried off to attend to the casualty.

Henry Alton was quickly alive to the situation. There was quite a kerfuffle out there in the waiting room, and he seized his chance. Deftly nudging the door closed, he buttoned up his shirt, grabbed the doctor's hat and coat from their nearby peg and slipped them on.

The surgery window was small, but Alton had little trouble squeezing his spindly frame through it. The doc's coat was long enough to cover his prison-issue trousers to below the knees, and he buttoned it up and tilted the brim of the hat down over his head as he walked briskly to the gates.

His luck was in. The gates stood open, as a grocery van had just driven in, and the driver was rabbiting away to the guard about the best bets for four aways on that week's pools coupon. Alton strode by unnoticed and out into the wide, open spaces beyond. It had taken less than two minutes, and he'd acted on impulse, with no clue as to how he'd get away from there nor where he'd be heading. London was the destination which sprang to mind: he had friends there – or as near to friends as he was likely to get - who he hoped would help him. But London was some distance away.

He dug his hands into the coat pockets. More good luck: there was money in one of them. He hauled it out and counted it: a half-crown, two shillings and a threepenny bit. Four-and-ninepence wouldn't get him far, but it was better than nothing.

His first objective was to put some distance between himself and the prison. He'd reached the edge of the village, and a gaggle of people were hanging around a bus stop. Alton joined them, and within minutes a bus appeared, bound for some place he'd never heard of. When the conductor came along, Alton asked for a single ticket to the place he'd seen on the bus's destination board, hoping it wouldn't cost more than the little he had. Fortunately, it only cost a couple of bob, and the conductor didn't so much as glance at him as he issued the ticket.

Alton chanced a look round at his fellow passengers, relieved that no-one was paying him any attention. It didn't take him long to clock the two young women who sat farther up the bus and across the aisle from him. They were nattering obliviously away, one with dark, curly hair, the other with blonde hair down over her shoulders. Alton preferred blondes. He couldn't see their faces but reckoned they'd be reasonably pretty. Both were a bit on the plump side, but he didn't mind that. Didn't mind anything, 'cause it had been so long. He decided to get off the bus when they did, follow them. They'd probably split up, and that'd leave just the one…

But no – *no*. His breathing had started to labour, and he was getting odd looks from the old dragon seated across from him, so he pulled himself up sharply. By now, they'd have discovered he was missing and sounded a general alert. He needed to concentrate on getting away, far away. Everything else could wait. He forced himself to think, to forget about the women.

The bus was passing through another anonymous village, and Alton noticed a station and, even better, a goods yard. He got off at the next stop, glad that he wasn't the only one to do so. Once the rest had trailed away, he looked round to make sure no-one else was in sight, clambered down the embankment and across to the goods yard. An engine was shunting trucks around, and Alton climbed into an empty one. He pulled the canopy over him, the warmest he'd felt all day.

He must have dozed off then, because suddenly the train was moving. Alton hoped his run of luck was about to continue, and he'd end up at some main line station. But he wasn't moving for long. The train slowed almost immediately, and he guessed they were pulling into another siding. Then the trucks clanked to a halt, jarring him completely awake, and he could hear the engine which had raised his hopes puffing treacherously away.

Alton waited a short while before emerging from beneath the canopy. He saw buildings in the distance and a platform a hundred yards or so down the line, a village halt or station. As he scrambled down from the truck, a man walked out on to the platform, and Alton assumed from the cap and uniform he wore that he was the stationmaster. He had an air of authority about him as he strolled away in the opposite direction, pausing to inspect the contents of a flowerbed.

Alton took the opportunity to slip across the line and sneak down the side of the track, out of the man's line of vision should he suddenly turn and look up. There was a wicket gate to his left, and he went through it to find himself on the other side of the station building. He peered through the window into a ticket office, spotted a coat hanging on the back of a door and immediately wondered if the coat might contain a wallet. There was one way to find out.

He hurried into the building and tried the door to the office. It was locked. A heavy footfall sounded behind him, and Alton swung round in alarm to find the stationmaster looming over him.

"Up to no good, are you, my lad?" he boomed.

The man was taller than Alton and had the air of an old serviceman, and Alton was certain he'd come off worse in a scrap: he always had, which was why he studiously avoided them. He took the one option open to him and turned and ran, chancing to look back only when he reached the road. The stationmaster stood in the doorway of the building, shaking a fist at him.

Alton cursed himself for not having been on the ball. The man struck him as someone able to give a decent description, particularly once he learned about the escape, either from the radio or a newspaper. Alton told himself he had to obtain a change of clothes as a matter of urgency.

The village – another name he didn't recognise – was a quarter of a mile along the road. The main street was quiet, although it contained a number of small shops. If his luck held, he'd be able to nick some food as well.

But clothes were his first concern, and as he ambled along the street, he came upon a shop which should serve his purpose. It was an emporium, crammed with all kinds of miscellaneous goods, and as he crept in, Alton noticed a rack labelled 'Gents' Clothing' halfway down the narrow, cluttered aisle.

A spotty youth sat at the cash desk, across from Alton's intended destination, but fortunately his attention was elsewhere, as he was engaged in a private telephone conversation, probably without the absent owner's permission. A quick look round informed Alton that there was no-one else in the store.

"Oh, come on, Sandra," the youth whined. "We can get the last bus back home. There's this film on at the Palace in town, and when I seen what it was I fought of you, 'cause it's called *Nuffink But The Best,* and I want to take you to see it, 'cause I fink you're the best, and it's a really good film – well, I'm sure it is – and I promise I'll buy you a bag of chips afterwards…"

After what? Alton thought, grinning lasciviously, as he lifted a jacket, trousers and cap from the rack, hoping that Sandra would hold out for a couple of minutes more, so that he could make his way out unobserved. She did, and he wondered colourfully if her resistance would finally end in the Palace's back row later that evening. He silently wished the youth the best of luck, wished he might be in his place.

His next stop was at the village hall's public conveniences. There was a sliver of soap at the sink, and he sluiced his hands and face before donning his new garments in a cubicle. The jacket was tight under his arms, the trousers short in the leg and the cap too big, but that didn't worry him, and he stuffed the doctor's hat and coat in a litter bin outside.

Feeling slightly less conspicuous in his new togs, he walked farther along the street, where he came upon a Wavy Line grocer's shop. The counter was at the far end, and the woman behind it gossiping loudly and nineteen to the dozen to a customer, while slicing up some ham and putting together her order.

Alton slipped out of her view and crammed a few items into his pockets, distracted as a woman walked in, high heels clicking on the stone floor. He watched open-mouthed as she approached the counter. She wore a jacket over a tight skirt, and he guessed she'd be a clerk or a secretary. He caught himself breathing heavily again, almost gasping, and fought to tear his gaze away. When he found he couldn't stuff any more into his pockets, he ducked out of the shop and along the street. A church clock struck five, and the light was already starting to fade. Just in case anyone had clocked him furtively leaving the shop, he turned down the next street, which looked as if it might lead out of the village.

Someone had left a bike propped against some railings. Checking swiftly around to ensure he hadn't been observed, Alton took it and rode away. It was almost falling apart, a creaky old sit-up-and-beg, but it would serve his purpose in getting him to a main line station and then somehow on to London, where there lived a couple of family acquaintances who would (he hoped) take him in. He didn't particularly like them and knew the feeling was mutual, but they were about his only option.

He rode several miles through the countryside before the chain snapped, sending him tumbling on to the grass verge. It was practically dark, not a dwelling in sight, and Alton swore volubly – his mother would have been scandalised – realising he'd have to spend the night out of doors.

He'd been passing a stretch of woodland, so he wheeled the offending bike in and abandoned it, before walking deeper into the wood. He pitched down against the bole of a tree and wolfed down some of the stolen food, conscious that news of his escape would have made the evening paper and probably radio and even television. His one advantage was that no-one could possibly have tracked him to his current location, the disadvantage being that he didn't know where he was himself.

But the pursuit would be out in force. He was a convicted rapist, whom the judge had branded a danger to women. What the old fool had failed to understand was that none of it had been his fault: the women he'd assaulted had been asking for it. No-one – apart from Mother, who'd labelled them all jezebels – had understood, and her devoted Henry had been sentenced to a long stretch in prison, interrupted by that morning's daring escape.

Alton didn't feel so daring now. He'd gorged all the food he'd stolen from the Wavy Line shop – he should have taken more – and washed it down with a bottle of Corona, finishing with a loud belch before getting up and staggering further into the dense wood, completely hidden from the road.

Luck smiled on him again when he came upon a tumbledown shack, long abandoned, went inside and made himself as comfortable as he could before falling into an exhausted sleep. He was awoken in the early hours by the sound of rain drumming on the roof and then water seeping through and steadily soaking him. He huddled in a corner, managing to keep as dry as he could, and slept uneasily for a while longer. Eventually the rain ceased.

He stumbled out of the shack to a cold, bright morning, his stomach growling for food. He walked, careless of the direction taken, because he was bound to emerge from the wood at some stage. Even so, after what seemed like several hours, he was beginning to despair when suddenly the trees thinned out, and he found himself not only in a lane, but one which was populated.

Across the lane stood several houses: a thatched cottage, then, some distance along a pair of bungalows and another cottage. The thatched cottage grabbed his attention. There was a looping gravelled drive on which, despite his view being hampered by a tall brambly hedge, he could make out a battered Land Rover parked outside the cottage's front door.

He wondered if the owner might have been obliging enough to have left the key in the ignition and had begun to cross the lane to test that hypothesis when the slamming of a door sent him scurrying back into the cover of the trees.

He watched as a man locked the cottage door and walked round to the driver's side of the vehicle. He was quite short and no youngster, but he looked in good shape, probably an ex-military man, and Alton knew he'd come off second best in a struggle. The man was carrying a holdall, which he slung on to the passenger seat before getting behind the wheel and driving away.

Because of the locked front door, Alton thought it reasonable to assume that there was no-one else at home. As a distant church clock struck ten, he crossed the lane and prowled round the house, checking each window and concluding that the house was empty.

Things were looking up. He slaked his thirst from a tap in the back garden, splashed his face and defecated in the bushes. As well as a small shed containing tools and a bicycle, there was some sort of summerhouse in the corner of the garden, which looked new, and the old boy had thoughtfully left a key under a flowerpot beside the door. Some people never learned.

Alton opened the door and went in. From the photographs on the walls, he learned that the old boy was ex-army, and the clutter on the desk told him he was probably writing his memoirs. Weren't they all? He found a disgusting pipe in the top drawer and some tobacco in a tin but resisted the urge to light up. In another drawer sat a half-empty packet of Lincoln biscuits. He bit into one: it was soft, but he didn't care because it was edible. He sat and chomped his way through the whole lot, conscious of the grunting noises he made while he ate. He found himself still desperately hungry and longed for a cooked meal, wouldn't have turned up his nose at prison fare. But he didn't plan to go back there.

Putting hunger aside, he was lifted by the discovery of another key, because he was sure it would gain him access to the house. He intended to try it right away, but weariness was beginning to overwhelm him. The chair behind the desk was cushioned and high-backed: to him, the last word in luxury. He scrunched down into it and was soon asleep.

He was awoken by the throaty growl of a bus out in the lane. The clock on the wall in front of him informed him that it was late afternoon. He heard light footsteps on the gravel, the sound of a door closing. It wasn't the old boy, and anyway he'd gone off in his Land Rover. His missus, then? And what if she went to a window and glimpsed him in here? He couldn't take that chance. With great reluctance, he left the summerhouse, locked it, pocketed the key and hid himself in the undergrowth.

He watched the house and saw someone at an upstairs window. Too young, surely, to be the old boy's missus? A daughter, perhaps? Should he try the key later, after dark? Although if it didn't work, the scraping in the lock might awaken her, and she'd have time to alert the cops.

Alton waited until darkness had fallen before letting himself carefully back into the summerhouse. He'd made little noise, but suddenly there she was, drawing the curtains across an upstairs window. He'd wait for her to go out the next day – surely, she would? – and try the house then.

If she happened to come back while he was in there…

He chuckled lewdly. Well, if she did, he could guarantee her a nice surprise.

18

On his arrival at the station the next morning, Neal went along to the DCI's office to report on progress. He was following up the Colin Trevis angle, while he'd set Dakers the task of identifying the young man who'd called into Brake's corner shop for the second time and left a blob of mud in the doorway. If he'd been present at a burial at the nearby cemetery the morning in question, they were on the way to tracking him down.

Pilling seemed satisfied with Neal's report, less so with having been compared to Inspector Clouseau in the film he'd gone to see at his wife's insistence the previous evening. But there was a hint of amusement in his manner. "And yes, DS Gallian. Thank you for recommending that film. I enjoyed watching it – I think."

Later that morning, Neal parked a little way down from Nadine Ellison's house. As he walked on to the drive and saw only the pristine Austin A40 parked outside the double garage, he guessed he'd find her alone. Which was a pity, as he'd be denied a chance to chat with Dale Corlett. He grinned, scolding himself for being so cynical.

Nadine Ellison promptly opened the door to his ring. "You're nice and early – oh!"

She took a step back on seeing who the caller was. She was dressed to the nines in an expensive beige two-piece and matching court shoes. He couldn't have said whether her stunning perfume was Givenchy or Chanel, but it was bound to be expensive.

Neal smiled his apology. "Acting DS Gallian, Mrs Ellison. You'll remember me from the other day."

She'd quickly overcome her surprise and had reverted to her customary cool and efficient self. "Of course. I take it you're here to inform me that you've found the man who killed the burglar?"

She stood holding the door, an expression of polite inquiry on her face. She was hoping it'd be a quick answer, because he could tell she was reluctant to let him in.

But Neal wasn't going to be turned away so easily. "It's another line of inquiry, Mrs Ellison, which I hope will lead us to Derek Medway's killer. May I ask if you knew a man named Colin Trevis?"

"Colin Trevis?" There'd been a flash of something – shock? panic? – in her eyes, and he had his answer. "Well – yes. Er, perhaps you'd better come in."

She stood aside to admit him, indicating for him to go through to the lounge. "Will this take long?" she asked, as she followed along behind him. "I'm expecting a friend to call. We're due to have lunch in High Wycombe."

"It'll be very brief," Neal assured her, as he took the armchair from his previous visit. He didn't think he'd need to guess at the friend's identity.

Nadine perched gingerly on the edge of the sofa opposite. She sat with her hands clasped in her lap, as if in prayer, and looked vague and perhaps a little anxious.

"We traced the gun which killed Derek Medway to Colin Trevis," Neal said. "And it's looking as if Trevis may have been Medway's accomplice in the burglary. Medway came away with less money than they'd expected, there was a quarrel and probably Trevis shot him. As you're no doubt aware, Trevis was killed a few weeks later in a wages van ambush that went wrong. Mrs Ellison, why I asked if you knew Trevis was because his daytime job was painting and decorating. I've heard that he'd done some work up this way and wondered if he might have worked for you or your husband at any time?"

Nadine had visibly relaxed, and Neal thought she'd guessed where he was going with this line of questioning. He wondered what she'd thought he'd been about to ask.

"Yes, he did," she replied. "He and Bernard seemed to get on well, and the work he did in the house and gallery couldn't be faulted. But I can't say that I liked him."

"Why was that?" Neal kept his tone deliberately light.

She looked uneasy. "Bernard was a good man, but he was far too trusting. He never seemed to notice the way Trevis looked at me – a way which would make most women feel uncomfortable."

Nadine hesitated, and Neal waited patiently, nodding for her to go on as soon as she was ready. She cleared her throat and continued.

"Every Monday night without fail, Bernard went out. It was some businessman's club in the city centre. I used to attend the annual banquet with him, as well as a few other gatherings. It was all very boring, but he seemed to enjoy it, God rest him. He must have mentioned it to Trevis, who put two and two together and realised I'd be in the house alone. He called on two occasions, the first when he made the excuse of having forgotten to pick up his toolbox. I was pleasant to him, offered him a drink, and he misread my gesture, became over-friendly and made several suggestive remarks. The second time, having insinuated himself into the house, he promptly propositioned me." She looked up, her eyes flashing angrily. "He didn't succeed, Sergeant. I rejected his crude advances and threatened to call the police. It was enough to see him off."

"He wasn't violent towards you in any way?"

"I certainly felt he was capable of violence, and I can assure you I was very frightened. But no, he didn't lay a finger on me. He was sensible enough to know that nobody would take his word against mine."

"Did you mention either incident to your husband?"

Nadine stared down at her hands, unable to look him in the eye. She shook her head briefly. "I felt – how can I put it? – almost sullied. I simply couldn't tell Bernard. I just wanted Trevis to finish his work and leave us alone."

"So, this happened when Trevis worked here. When was that?"

"Late September through to the end of the October. He was good at his work. Bernard settled up, and that was the last I saw of Trevis." She looked up ruefully. "I'm glad poor Bernard wasn't around when Trevis was killed in that incident. He'd never have lived it down, for it to be known that he'd been so friendly with a common criminal."

Neal reflected on how Nadine's information had given the case a new complexion. He could see Col Trevis at the centre of it. Medway had always been marked out as the victim. Angered by Nadine's rejection of him and with the knowledge that the proceeds from Bernard's recent sale had been safely deposited with the bank, Trevis had set up Medway for the bungled break-in, got rid of Bernard and arranged Medway's death and disappearance once they were away from the scene.

But it seemed as if Bernard Ellison might have had the last laugh.

"The money from your husband's sale?" Neal asked. "He'd put it in the safe. As it was a large amount, wouldn't he have been given it in the form of a cheque?"

Nadine shook her head. "Bernard always insisted on cash. As you say, it was a large amount, and on the way to his club on the Monday evening, he took the majority with him to the bank and stored it in the night safe."

"Which meant that Medway got away with very little?"

"No more than a couple of hundred," she replied with a prim smile.

The last laugh indeed – but at a dreadful cost.

At that moment the front doorbell jangled, and Nadine was immediately on her feet. "Have we finished, Sergeant? Er, my -?"

"Yes, Mrs Ellison. Thank you. You've been most helpful."

He rose slowly to his feet but hung back deliberately. Nadine was already out of the room and marching purposefully down the hallway. He heard the door open and her voice almost a whisper, the words inaudible. Neal imagined her pressing a silencing finger to her lips.

He ambled out of the lounge in time to meet her ushering Dale Corlett, resplendently clean-cut in blazer, white flannels, polo shirt and moccasins, down the hallway.

"Good morning, Mr Corlett," Neal greeted him.

"Ah, DS Gallian." Corlett's tone was casual as, unfortunately, he'd been forewarned of Neal's presence. "I've just come to collect Nadine. We're in a bit of a hurry…"

"Yes, High Wycombe. Mrs Ellison told me. I won't keep you." But the temptation to make the ultra-smooth Corlett wriggle proved too great. "I believe I saw you last night, Mr Corlett?"

"Oh?" The man was immediately on his guard.

"Yes. I called in briefly at the Blue Dahlia."

"Ah, of course. Loretta mentioned you'd called."

It had been a spirited attempt at recovery but earned Corlett the evil eye from Nadine.

"Loretta Taine?" Her words dripped venom.

Corlett was wriggling alright, the legacy of a guilty conscience. "Er, yes, DS Gallian called to interview her about a gun sold to one of the Dahlia's customers a while back. Loretta felt she ought to report the matter to me."

"Miss Taine was very helpful," Neal put in.

Nadine turned her frosty stare on him. "I'm sure."

"Do you visit the Blue Dahlia often, Mr Corlett?" Neal asked, guessing the state of play from Corlett's last sentence.

"Well, in a way." Corlett chuckled nervously, alert to the return of Nadine's careful scrutiny. "I -er, manage it, you see. Sam Diamond's the owner – a prominent local businessman. He's winding down towards retirement these days – actually holidaying on some island in the Caribbean at present – and I manage the day to day running."

"I've heard of him," Neal replied mildly. "By all accounts, a hard taskmaster." *And another of those dodgy operators we've never been able to bring to book,* he didn't add.

"Certainly keeps me on my toes. Even phones in while on holiday. No rest for the wicked, eh?"

This was beginning to sound a mite too jolly, and Neal changed tack. "Might you have known Colin Trevis, then, Mr Corlett? He seems to have been a good customer of the Blue Dahlia."

"So I'd heard." Corlett's tone was even, and Neal could tell the question hadn't ruffled him. "But that was before my time there, DS Gallian. I've been manager for just over a year." He turned to Nadine. "Er, I rather think we should be -?"

Neal smiled placatingly. "My apologies. I *am* keeping you. It's time I was on my way too."

He doubted they'd quarrel with that. Nadine's expression had thawed out as she walked him to the door, and Corlett had offered a hand, which Neal had shaken, finding the palm slightly moist in his grasp.

"Do keep me informed of progress, Sergeant," Nadine gushed, as she opened the door.

"I will, Mrs Ellison. Thank you."

From where he'd left the Anglia along the road, Neal had a good view of Dale Corlett assiduously hovering over Nadine as she got into the passenger seat. He watched them drive off. They couldn't get away quickly enough. He wasn't a betting man, but he'd have wagered Loretta Taine's name would feature somewhere in their conversation.

Neal found himself distrusting Dale Corlett even more. He guessed he was two-timing Nadine with Loretta, and that she had her suspicions. Somehow, he couldn't bring himself to feel sorry for her. But he couldn't help wondering if, attractive though she was, Corlett wasn't more interested in her money.

19

Henry Alton awoke after a fitful night's sleep. He felt ravenous for food and exhausted after his adventures of the previous day, numb with both the cold and his perpetual fear of falling foul of the police. He carefully surveyed the scene from the summerhouse window. The girl had drawn back all the curtains, and Alton had a good view into the downstairs room, where she was shrugging into her coat. Clearly, she was going out, quite possibly to work.

He heard the approach of the bus and the slamming of the front door. The engine gurgled throatily as it slowed to a halt and, taking a chance, Alton left the summerhouse and crept round to the wicket gate at the side of the cottage. Through the bushes which screened it from the lane, he saw the back view of her getting on it. She was wearing slacks and a sheepskin coat, her blonde hair tied back in a ponytail. He lost himself for a moment in a pleasing, sordid daydream, and by the time he opened his eyes, the bus had driven away. Alton noticed that the old boy in the Land Rover hadn't returned the previous night and resolved to stay alert, as he supposed he might reappear at any time.

He hurried back to the summerhouse and grabbed hold of the key he'd left in a drawer. He crossed the lawn and made to push it into the lock. It missed and fell to the ground. Cursing, he snatched it up, knowing that it must fit, had to, and as he finally wriggled it into the lock and turned it, he let out an impulsive whoop of delight. Immediately, he fell silent, looking around guiltily. But unless someone had been passing in the lane at that moment, it was likely he wouldn't have been heard.

Suddenly, Alton found himself in the kitchen. He tugged open a door which gave on to a pantry, stacked with tins of food. There was part of a loaf in the bread bin, and he hauled it out, then went to the refrigerator and grabbed the remains of a pork pie and some cheese. So much food, and Henry Alton was going to eat it all. His stomach gurgled excitedly in full agreement.

Then common sense kicked in. He found a knife and cut two slices of bread, slathering them with butter. He guzzled water from the tap over the sink and signed off with a massive, satisfied belch, paused and waited for a moment, but no-one could have heard.

Then he wandered at leisure through the house. In the bathroom, he took an involuntary step back, gasping at the sight in the mirror of his grubby, unshaven face, and his sparse, unruly hair sprouting in all directions.

Alton washed his hands and dried them on his trousers, looked through the contents of the bathroom cabinet. There was the old boy's shaving kit, which he forced himself to leave alone, despite his longing to use it, some bottles of cologne, nail scissors and hairbrushes.

Her room had a dainty quilt on the bed. Alton examined the items on her dressing table: a comb, a brush, bottles of perfume. He ran his hands over her clothes hanging in the wardrobe, wrapped one of her stockings round his fingers, experiencing a violent rush of pleasure, making him fight to contain himself.

That had to be enough: he mustn't allow himself to get carried away. And yet thoughts of the girl filled his mind, how she'd looked so young and unspoiled, not like those jezebels, those cunning, posturing women who'd been far from young, who'd fully deserved everything they'd got.

And of course, the old boy might be back at any time. What if he returned during the day? Well, then he'd have to stay hidden and nick the Land Rover after dark, or otherwise break the flimsy padlock on the door of the small garden shed and ride off on the bike – which had to be hers – that he'd seen in there.

But first, and most necessary of all, there was food. In passing, he noticed a decanter of scotch on the sideboard. There were two empty milk bottles in the kitchen, and Alton took one and half-filled it from the decanter, anticipating the illicit buzz it would give him. For Mother wouldn't allow it in the house, warning him that it was bad for him, that it would make him think and do evil things, and she didn't want her Henry led into temptation.

He returned to the summerhouse, having taken care to lock the back door. He put the key back in the drawer, ate every last crumb of the food he'd stolen, grunting contentedly as he chewed; drank all the scotch, felt his head spin pleasurably and promptly fell asleep in the old boy's comfortable padded chair.

*

Towards the end of that afternoon, Jill Westmacott thanked the driver and got off the bus, walked up the drive and let herself into the house. As she hung up her coat, she reflected on the jobs she'd completed that day. She'd hung the new bedroom curtains in the flat and had put a coat of gloss on some of the connecting doors after Neal had undercoated them the previous week.

He'd called in for a sandwich and a cup of tea that lunchtime, and they'd spent a contented hour together. Her next plan was to choose some new carpet for the sitting room. He'd been okay with that, offering to pay for it, but she insisted on doing that from her savings. They'd had a good-natured argument over the matter, had agreed to pay half each and sealed the arrangement with a kiss. Neal had promised to phone her at Briar Hedge that evening, as he'd be working late. Mr Pilling was likely to be out all day and would want a progress report on the current investigation when he got back to his office.

Jill was looking forward to spending the weekend in Neal's company. He was so busy at work, trying to track down a killer from over two years ago and hoping it would lead him to the man he called the Face. She was determined to treat him to a day out on the Saturday and drive him to Bournemouth. And *she'd* do the driving, get herself used to being behind the wheel of his old but reliable Consul. The Central Gardens would be starting to take shape, and she'd have the chance to wander round Beale's department store. Then on Sunday, she'd cook a roast dinner for him and Uncle Lam, and he could put his feet up, read the paper and have a snooze if he wanted, just like her uncle.

She ensured the house was secure, drew all the curtains and made some tea. There was a strange, earthy smell in the kitchen, which she couldn't place, and she wondered if the farmer had sprayed something unpleasant on the fields behind the cottage. They were low on milk, and Jill wrote a note to put in the empty bottle, asking the milkman to leave two pints. She stood the bottle out on the doorstep, staring down at it for a moment, because she'd been sure there'd been two empties that morning.

In the sitting room with a cup of tea, she noticed that Uncle Lam had rather gone to town on the scotch. She knew he'd missed her, those six weeks she'd been in Kenya, but he really ought to cut down. She'd have a word with him when he got back the following day.

Returning to the kitchen to pour herself a second cup, Jill decided she'd have a snack. There'd been the remains of a pork pie in the fridge but, try as she might, she couldn't find it. Had she eaten it the previous night? She didn't think so, but concluded that she must have done, because it wasn't there. She wondered fleetingly if she was going mad.

The answer to that was – probably. Because all that occupied her mind were the preparations for their wedding in September, the work she was planning for their wonderful flat, and above all else Neal. He was patient, kind, strong – yet at the same time, she believed, terribly vulnerable, still somehow haunted by the past. She was sure there were things he'd never told her – although she knew he would when the time was right. She wondered if there was any girl in the world as happy as she was.

And that was why she needed to concentrate on the everyday things, like managing the housekeeping. It would be her responsibility, so that he could concentrate on his job.

She was startled out of her reverie by an authoritative-sounding knock at the front door. Before answering it, she peeped round the hallway curtain to see who was there. With a sigh, she opened the door.

The caller was the Braxbury policeman, Sergeant Tomkins, a man who was a long way from being her favourite person. He stood self-importantly on the doorstep, resplendent in uniform, gleaming boots and repulsive, pencil-thin moustache.

"Good evening, Miss Westmacott." His probing eyes inspected her from toe to top. "Your uncle in?"

"He's away overnight, Sergeant Tomkins. He'll be back tomorrow."

"I see. I'm here to advise you to keep your doors locked, miss. There's an escaped convict on the loose from Grantonwood prison."

"Yes, I heard about it on the radio earlier."

"He may be in this area. There've been a trail of thefts and a possible sighting not many miles from here. All the police in the county are on the alert."

Tomkins' booming voice promised reassurance. However, Jill didn't feel the words 'alert' and 'Tomkins' necessarily belonged together.

"I shall certainly take care, Sergeant," she promised crisply. "Thank you."

But Tomkins hadn't finished. "I -er, hear you're engaged to that young Gallian, and that he's back with the police?"

"Yes, he's with Oxford CID."

"Ah. One of the whizz-kids, then." Tomkins' tone was disparaging, and Jill took it as an insult. Neal and the sergeant had had a run-in a few months back, when Neal had been a civilian, and, as she recalled, Tomkins hadn't had the best of it.

"Neal works very hard, Sergeant Tomkins," she replied acidly.

Tomkins missed the implied sarcasm, his eyes too busy appraising her again. "Oh, I don't doubt it, Miss Westmacott," he leered. "Don't doubt it at all. Remember, I'm just up the road in Braxbury, if you should need me."

But Jill had already closed the door firmly on his parting invitation. If she should *need* him, indeed!

Still, she had to admit, he had a point, and it persuaded her to go round the whole house again and check windows and doors.

Back in the sitting room, she leapt, startled, as the phone in the hallway jangled stridently, didn't know what prompted her to run through to answer it. But it was Neal, and she immediately felt calmer. He'd said he would phone: he was just about to go out, something to do with the investigation, and he'd wanted to check up on her before he left the station. He sounded anxious: it was possible that an escaped convict might be in the vicinity.

Jill replied that she'd just had a visit from Sergeant Tomkins, who'd advised her to lock all her doors and close the windows. She assured Neal that she'd done that but knew he'd continue to fret about her. To set his mind at rest, she responded with a brightness she couldn't quite feel, joshing him that he worried too much, and she was more than capable of looking after herself. He sounded in a bit of a hurry, so she said her tea was in the oven and cheerfully sent him off on his investigation.

And once she'd replaced the receiver, she wished she hadn't.

But what was there to worry about? The house was secure, and she felt perfectly safe…

*

Henry Alton had been lurking behind the house during the copper's visit. He'd just locked the summerhouse and returned the key to its customary position beneath the pot. The key to the house nestled in his pocket.

He didn't hear everything the copper said, but enough to realise they were on to him and closing in.

It would soon be dark. He'd return to the house then, seek out more food and some money before setting off.

And of course, before he left, there was the girl.

Emboldened by the scotch, he promised himself that he mustn't forget the girl…

20

On his return to the station that afternoon, Neal drew Tom Wrightson aside to ask for some information, after which he went along to his office to find Sally Dakers waiting for him. He could tell by the look on her face that she'd had a fruitful morning.

Dakers had managed to identify two likely young men who'd attended Miss Wayfleet's funeral on 6th March. They were cousins, both related to the dead woman and both in their early twenties: Terry Arden worked for a local builder, and Mark Jevons was a bank clerk. Arden lived in Marston and Jevons in Headington, so either of them might have carried out the shop hold-ups on the way home from visits to Miss Wayfleet's house in Rose Hill.

"I called on their mothers this morning, once the boys were at work," Sally said. "I didn't get far with Mrs Arden. Her main concern was that some of her aunt's money would find its way to her, because the old lady had died without making a will, and there'd be no justice if it didn't because she and her sister had been the only living relatives. She seemed to carry the weight of the world on her shoulders, and I didn't want to make her suspicious. Terry didn't go back to Miss Wayfleet's after the burial. He needed to get back home to change for work, and his mum felt he'd have been long gone by the time the 'incident' took place near the cemetery gates.

"I decided to leave it there, and quite honestly she couldn't wait for me to go."

Her sister, Mrs Jevons, however, had been another matter altogether. She was a busy, cheerful woman of fifty, with an elderly mother-in-law to look after and a husband who was a traveller for a confectionery firm and hardly ever at home. As she sat Sally down and poured her a succession of cups of tea, she rattled blithely on, and as a bonus gave her more information about her nephew Terry Arden than Sally could ever have hoped to have extracted from his mother.

"Poor Aunt Honoria was ill for so long, but with my Ted away so much and Ted's mum needing more or less constant care, I couldn't get over there anywhere near as often as I'd have liked. But our Mark's been a treasure, God bless him. These last six months, he's been to visit her at least once a week. He's *such* a good boy. Got *such* a responsible job in the bank. The manager even sends him out to look after one of the village branches, just him on his own, he's got so much faith in him…"

Once Mrs Jevons had paused to take a breath, Sally had grasped the opportunity to ask if Mark was close to his cousin Terry? There'd been an incident near the cemetery gates, round about the time Miss Wayfleet's burial had taken place – a lady's handbag had been snatched, and the thief had run off. Had Terry and Mark left the cemetery together? She supposed they'd both have had to get back to work. Was there a chance the boys might have noticed anything? Someone running away in a hurry, for example?

"Well, Mark didn't come back to Aunt Honoria's house, dear. And he never said anything about witnessing any incident or seeing somebody making off in a hurry. If he had, knowing our Mark, he'd have gone straight to the police. But no, he had to get back to the bank in the city centre, and he certainly wouldn't have left with Terry. The boys really don't have a lot in common. Terry's always been a *bit* wild, down at the pub a lot with his darts team. Not the way me and Ted have brought up our Mark. But then, Terry's not had it easy, bless him. Joan, my sister, has had a struggle to bring him up, 'cause her husband walked out when Terry was small."

"So, you don't think Terry would have visited his aunt after work as often as Mark did?"

Sally knew the question might well have made Mrs Jevons suspicious of her motive, but fortunately she didn't see it that way, screwing up her face in a dismissive gesture.

"Well, our Joan would have asked him to, I'm sure, but Terry's a different kettle of fish from Mark. He'd more likely have had other plans for his evenings, out chasing girls if he wasn't playing darts. I'm not sure how often he went round there, but it'd have been as well if he hadn't, because Aunt Honoria – well, she could be a bit *awkward*, you know, the way old people often are." Mrs Jevons leaned across the table and lowered her voice to a conspiratorial whisper. "She kept all her money in a tin *under her bed.*

Our Mark tried to persuade her to invest it in the bank where it'd be safe. But she refused to let him do it. It had always been kept there, she said, and that's where it would remain. Anyway, once she'd died, Mark handed it over to the solicitor. I suppose in the end it'll come to me and Joan, as her closest relatives, but, oh dear me, what a fuss Auntie used to make."

Mrs Jevons had chattered on to the extent that Sally had left with her ears ringing and had had to ask to use the loo before she went on account of all the cups of tea she'd consumed in the line of duty.

But Neal, having listened to the edited version of his WDC's morning, was delighted. "One of them's got to be our boy," he concluded. "But which one? What's your opinion, Sally?"

She immediately perked up at him addressing her by her Christian name as well as being asked for her opinion, and her a lowly DC and a woman. It made a difference from being asked to fetch and carry for lazy, overweight male colleagues.

"Well, Sarge, without a doubt Terry Arden's a bit of a lad. But I felt Mrs Jevons was rather prejudiced. And she made her Mark sound like a candidate for sainthood. He just sounded too good to be true."

"So, you think we should keep an open mind?"

"Definitely. Do you want them both brought here, Sarge?"

"Yes, but one at a time. Once again, WDC Dakers, good work. Now, grab your coat because we've got a call to make before we proceed any further with Messrs Arden and Jevons."

Sally lifted her raincoat off the peg and followed Neal out into the corridor. Taff Thomas happened to be walking past.

"Oh, Taff?" Neal called after him. "Have you seen Mal Brady at all this afternoon?"

"He's along in the canteen, Gally," came the reply. "I'm on my way there now. Want me to wake him up?"

"Please. And fire him in this direction if you will."

"It'll be my pleasure."

As they waited for Brady, Neal remembered that he had a phone call to make, excused himself and dashed back into his office. Sally grinned knowingly after his departing back: there were no prizes for guessing who he was about to ring.

Mal Brady rumbled into view a couple of minutes later, not looking best pleased for having had his hibernation curtailed. As he arrived, Neal emerged from the office.

"Ah, Mal. Good to see you. Busy day?"

"Feet are ruddy killing me, Gally," Brady whined. "That was the first time I got to sit down all day. The DCI nabbed me before I went out – had me running about all over flippin' Oxford."

"Sounds as if he's about to make you his right-hand man," Neal replied with a grin, knowing that Pilling was simply intent on keeping his less-than-enthusiastic colleague gainfully employed.

"Huh, some hopes."

"Okay." Neal's tone was suddenly brisk. "I've got a job for the three of us now. But before we go, Mal, what's the word on the Blue Dahlia? Is it reckoned to be doing well?"

Brady was suddenly in his element. "Yeah, it's doing okay, but some have their doubts about Sam Diamond taking a back seat. It's not the goldmine it was when he was there day to day, and he's on his second manager in a couple of years."

"Ask around some more, will you?"

"Sure thing." Mal followed Neal and Sally out into the yard. "What's happening now, then, Gally? We bringing someone in?"

"A suspect?" Sally Dakers couldn't keep the eagerness out of her tone.

"Let's say it's someone who'll help with our inquiries."

"Same thing, then," Brady mumbled, as they got in the car, Dakers, as the junior colleague, yielding the front seat to her esteemed colleague.

Neal parked the unmarked Anglia round the corner from Gloria Trevis' house and turned in his seat to brief the others.

"We're looking for Micky Parkin, a lad in his early twenties and a cousin of the late Colin Trevis. According to the reliable source sitting alongside me," he acknowledged Brady with a nod, "Micky's holed up with Col's widow. I heard someone moving around upstairs when I was there yesterday, and I'd guess it was him. Uncle Tom tells me there's a side alley at the end of the row, which leads round the backs of the houses and out into the neighbouring street. I'll call at the front, which means he may well do a runner out the back. I want you two round there to nab him if he does."

Sally Dakers was looking anxious, and Mal Brady turned majestically to reassure her. "Better let me take the lead on this one, love. I've been in similar situations before. You hold the bracelets at the ready, and I'll make the arrest."

Neal struggled to keep a straight face. "That's it, Dakers. Best let DC Brady take the lead."

"Watch and learn, love," Mal advised her smugly. "Watch and learn."

They got out of the car, and Neal sent them off to take up their positions, Brady, a head shorter than his female colleague, striding confidently out in front. He gave them a couple of minutes, then walked across and knocked at the front door. Within seconds, it was flung open to reveal Gloria Trevis, aggressively barring the doorway. "You again?" she snarled. "What is it now?"

"Mrs Trevis. I believe you have a lodger staying here?"

"What if I have?"

"Micky Parkin?"

Her reply was guarded. "He stays here from time to time."

"Is he here now?"

"Already left. He works nights up at Pressed Steel."

"It's four o'clock, and he won't be due in until at least seven. Sounds a bit too keen if you ask me. Mind if I have a word with him?"

"Only if you've got a warrant."

Neal's tone hardened. "This is a murder inquiry, Mrs Trevis. Want me to arrest you for obstruction?"

Gloria Trevis stood aside with bad grace. As Neal passed her and started up the stairs, she shrieked an ear-piercing warning.

"Micky! It's the filth! Get out quick!"

On hearing scrambling sounds from the bedroom on the landing, Neal took the stairs two at a time. He flung open the door to glimpse a slightly built, dark-haired figure in a lumberjack shirt disappearing through the open window on to the pitched roof of the kitchen.

He got to the window as Parkin leapt off the roof on to the scrubby lawn, stumbling only slightly as he picked himself up.

"Brady! Dakers!" Neal yelled. "He's coming your way!"

He watched as Mal Brady, signalling for Dakers to stand back, marched self-importantly forward as Parkin ran towards him down the garden path. He raised a commanding hand, reminding Neal of a constable directing traffic (*if only he was,* he thought).

"Michael Parkin, I'm a police officer, and I'm placing you – *ooofff!*"

Undeterred by the warning, the fleeing Parkin barged into Mal and sent him tumbling to land on his backside on the grass with a dull squelch.

Watch and learn... With a sigh, Neal turned, raced downstairs past a smirking Gloria and out through the rear door. Brady was slowly getting to his feet, and Parkin making a bid for freedom along the back path.

Neal watched as Sally Dakers gave chase, her flapping raincoat seeming to lend her wings. He reached the garden gate in time to see her bring down Parkin with a flying tackle, land on top, winding him, recite the statutory warning and cuff his hands behind his back.

Neal overtook the shuffling Brady. "Out of puff, are you, Mal?"

"Oh, give it a rest, Gally," Mal scowled.

Neal wasn't the type to rub it in: he'd never known any of his colleagues, himself included, who hadn't been made to look foolish at one time or another. "Better get out of that coat before we get back to the nick," he advised. "People might think you've had an accident."

He walked up to where Dakers stood proudly clutching the arm of a wretched-looking Parkin.

"Let's take him back," Neal said. "You can book him, Sally – resisting arrest and assaulting a police officer for starters. He's all yours."

"Right, Sarge." It was her first arrest as a CID officer, and she stood with eyes gleaming and face aglow. *Watch and learn, Mal,* he thought, as a subdued Brady limped up behind him, gracious enough to offer Sally a nod of approbation.

"Oh, and WDC Dakers?"

"Yes, Sarge?"

"Your slip's showing."

21

Darkness fell early that evening, and Jill was in a quandary. She prepared some food for an early supper and sat picking at it with very little appetite. Silly little suspicions kept niggling her. The half of pork pie which had been in the fridge: she really couldn't remember having eaten it, and it had definitely been there after Uncle Lam had left. She was sure there'd been more bread in the bread bin than there actually was, and she never cut it *that* untidily, and she could have sworn there'd been two milk bottles to put out rather than one. Then there was the level of scotch in Uncle Lam's decanter. He enjoyed a drink but had never been what she'd call a heavy drinker.

It was a horrendous thought but, try as she might, she couldn't chase it away. *Had someone been in the house?*

Her thoughts leapt immediately to Sergeant Tomkins' warning about the escaped convict. But surely, he couldn't be *here*? There were no signs of a break-in, she'd made sure all doors were locked when she'd gone out, all windows fastened. Surely, it couldn't be possible?

But the idea had taken root. *If* he was in the house, might he still be here? There was one way to find out. And if there was one quality living in the country and often being alone in the house had instilled in Jill, it was a certain amount of courage. She went round the house with a poker at the ready and checked in every cupboard and wardrobe, every conceivable hiding place.

And found nothing. She scolded herself for being ridiculous – *of course he couldn't have got in here* – sat down again and continued worrying.

Her next decision was to phone Neal. When he'd contacted her earlier, however, he'd said he was going out on an investigation. Might he be back by now? Could she leave a message for him to come over? For anyone? That nice WPC Yvonne, perhaps? Even phone Sergeant Tomkins, just three miles away in Braxbury? But no, certainly not Tomkins. Her pride wouldn't allow it.

And she couldn't do it anyway. She was appalled by the thought that she'd sound so feeble. She'd be letting herself and him down. When they were married, Neal would need someone reliable to come home to, not some weak-kneed, anxious woman who was scared of her own shadow.

Jill had got as far as picking up the receiver on the hallstand. Now, she set it down purposefully, went back to the sitting room, took up a book and tried to read.

*

Henry Alton had decided to move on that evening. It wouldn't surprise him if the copper came back, and he needed to get away from the area as quickly as he could. But it would be good to get his hands on some money, and he was sure there'd be some in the house.

He watched as the girl appeared at the upstairs windows to draw the curtains across. There was just enough natural light for him to make out her face. She'd let her hair down over her shoulders, and Alton visualised her slim body beneath that blouse. Suddenly, he found his breath coming in huge gasps, as he fantasized about taking her by the shoulders, spinning her round to face him, pinning her down on the bed in that very room where she was now, a silencing hand over her mouth…

He doubted the old boy would be back that evening, unless it was late. Alton intended to be well away by then, taking the bike from the shed in the absence of a motor vehicle. He grinned evilly as he fondled the back door key nestling in his pocket.

He'd make the most of the time left to him here.

*

Jill sat up with a start. She guessed she'd been dozing. The book she'd been reading was on the floor, and she realised it must have slipped off her lap. Perhaps that was what had awoken her. Her supper lay unfinished on the coffee table.

Suddenly, she heard another sound, like a key scratching in a lock. She peered out into the hallway. Could Uncle Lam have arrived home early?

But no, she'd surely have heard the deep growl of his Land Rover as it turned on to the drive. And anyway, wasn't tonight another of those endless reunion dinners, and he'd told her he definitely wouldn't be back until halfway through the next day?

In any case, the sound of the key wasn't coming from the front door. It was further away. For a moment, she sat there, astounded. *Someone was trying to unlock the kitchen door.*

Jill leapt to her feet, stood frozen for a moment, willing herself to move, to think. A door creaked open – yes, the kitchen door. Whoever had entered was now standing in the adjacent room.

Jill's path to the front door was clear. But it was locked, and he'd be upon her by the time she'd retrieved the key from the hallstand drawer and opened it – and then run the hundred yards to Mr Webb's house down the road.

She was already moving as she reasoned this out. She switched off the sitting room light to buy a few seconds and hurried into the hallway and up the stairs. She crossed the dark landing, found the phone on the desk in the study, lifted a receiver and dialled a number she knew well. The ringing seemed to go on endlessly, but at last a voice she recognised asked who was calling?

"Sergeant Wrightson?" Her voice was a parched, frightened whisper. "It's Jill Westmacott at Briar Hedge. *Please* – send Neal, or – or someone. Th-there's an intruder in the house…"

Tom's voice came back, calm and unhurried. "Where are you, miss? Downstairs?"

"Upstairs. In my uncle's study."

"Close the door and barricade yourself in if you can. Wedge a chair under the doorknob. We'll be there as soon as possible. I'll send Tomkins down from Braxbury as well – it won't take him many minutes to get there."

"Please – tell Neal." But Wrightson had broken the connection. So, how soon might someone get here? Tomkins was no more than three miles away. An unlikely saviour, and certainly not one she'd choose. But now it was a case of any port in a storm, and any pride she'd had, she'd gladly swallow…

Jill could hear the intruder creeping around downstairs. Her room lay across the landing, and there was a small bolt on the inside of her door. It might delay him long enough.

She stumbled over something as she moved away from the desk. It fell to the floor – something heavy. She stooped to retrieve it: Uncle Lam's ancient cricket bat. It was better than nothing.

As Jill picked it up, she heard an ominous creak. He was on the next to bottom stair. She made a dash for her room.

But it had been a higher tread which had made the noise. As she got to her doorway, she heard a rasping breath close behind her, felt it hot and numbing on her neck. He was there on the landing, immediately beside her.

Jill started to scream, but the noise was cut off as a heavy hand closed firmly over her mouth.

22

Tom Wrightson slammed down the receiver just as Sally Dakers was passing the desk to head for home. She could tell by the look on his face that something was very wrong.

"Dakers, has DS Gallian left?"

"Still in his office, Sarge. Shall I -?"

There was no need. *"Gally!"* he bawled. "Out here, quick!" Sally jumped involuntarily, never having heard such a stentorian voice since her school games mistress had harangued them for their various inconsistencies in the gym.

The office door immediately swung back, and Neal rushed out. "What's up, Tom?"

"Jill's just rung, lad. Someone's got into the house. I've told her to barricade herself in the study -."

"I'm on my way. Dakers – with me!"

"Yes, Sarge."

"Thomas and Hodgson are on patrol in the city centre," Wrightson called after them. "I'll get them to follow on. Light a fire under Tomkins, too."

But Neal was already out of the door, Sally panting to catch up with him. The little Anglia was already in motion as she bundled herself into the passenger seat. As she was jolted back in it, the siren was blaring and headlights scorching the road on full beam. Cornmarket, St Giles, Woodstock Road, all flashed past in what seemed like seconds.

Sally didn't know what to say, and in the end said nothing, because it wasn't the time for words. She watched him as he sat hunched over the wheel, his foot flat on the accelerator as he swerved in and out of the slowing traffic with the occasional warning blast on the horn. He drove as if the devil was on his back.

Where Neal was concerned, he was, for he was in the agony of turmoil. He feared he'd be too late to save Jill, for he'd guessed who the intruder must be, knew of his sordid history. *To have and to hold:* the words pounded in his brain. No – it wasn't to be for him. All his shame flooded back to taunt him: how he could and should have saved Clyde Holt.

But that wasn't all his shame, not by a long way. He recalled the meeting with Helen Holt the other evening, recalled his betrayal of the man who'd been his friend, the man who'd looked out for him, guided him through those early uncertain years. And how had Neal repaid him?

And this, what was happening now? Was it retribution? God's judgement upon him, waiting until now, when he was in this agony, before delivering the verdict on his sinfulness? But surely, if He was a God of mercy, *surely,* he couldn't let Neal be too late again? Not too late for *her.* He should have insisted – he had, but not assertively enough – that she should stay at the flat while her uncle was away. When he'd phoned her not very long ago – and he should have remarked upon it at the time – hadn't there been something in her voice, something she'd been holding back, and he hadn't bothered to question it? Because Jill knew her own mind. *"How many times have I stayed in that house on my own?"* she'd asked him, and he hadn't argued the point. *Please God, keep her safe,* he prayed again, again, a beseeching mantra, as he pushed the Anglia to its limit, unconscious to Sally Dakers beside him, observing him with compassion and with awe.

*

It was a mad, desperate switchback ride, overtaking every car on the road, although the traffic on the long stretch of the A40 was mercifully light.

Sally could hear a second police car some way behind. Thomas and Hodgson, she assumed, and in the Zephyr, a more powerful car. Neal heard it too, for it inspired him, if it were possible, to drive faster, desperate to arrive before them and save the girl he loved.

Sally was clinging to the arm rest by now, and the car's every sinew was rattling in protest, as they veered off the main road and plunged down Braxbury's High Street. A few minutes later, beyond the town, Neal finally slowed enough to turn into a driveway, the precipitate lurch to a halt spewing gravel everywhere.

There was another car by the front door, a Hillman with police markings, and a uniformed sergeant, who probably hadn't long arrived, buffeting ineffectually against the door in an effort to force his way in.

"You won't shift it – a waste of time," Neal barked, as he leapt out of the Anglia. "Come on, round the back. Move yourself! The door there's likely to be easier." He led the way, with Sally at his heels and the sergeant lumbering along behind.

The back door stood open, and Neal ran inside, flicking on every light switch as he passed. Sally heard another car skid to a halt, its blue light flashing, and she knew their back-up had arrived.

She followed Neal through to the front of the house, was right behind him as he hammered up the stairs. He halted abruptly in a doorway on the landing, and Sally, unable to pull up in time, clattered into the back of him, almost bouncing off.

Recovering, she peered over his shoulder and gasped at the sight of the body splayed out across the bed…

23

Jerry Rudd could sense a pay day beckoning. In the course of his wanderings, he accumulated useful information, and the snippet he'd recently picked up was worth going out of his way for. A car would have been useful. He didn't own one and had contemplated nicking one for the evening, but on reflection had decided that it wasn't worth the risk of getting pulled over.

He'd taken the train from Oxford. All it had cost had been a platform ticket, because once on the train he'd nipped along to hide in the loo as soon as the ticket inspector had arrived on the scene.

Jerry Rudd lived on his wits, prospered by keeping his eyes and ears open, and he had a memory for faces. It was part of the reason why he'd never needed to get himself a proper job. In this case, all it had taken had been a glimpse, a face he'd recognised from having seen it just the once. The bloke had been calling on a shop and had left a business card on the counter for the manager. Jerry, who'd been out for the day in a town which he hadn't visited before, some distance from home, was prowling around to see what goodies he could lift. He'd spotted it, clocked the bloke and swiped the card, with the idea that it might come in useful.

The next evening, he'd phoned the bloke's home number from a callbox – his landlady didn't have a phone, which was just as well, because calls could be traced to there. She was a decent old soul, half-blind and in the habit of leaving bits of money around the house, which helped pay for his phone calls and then some. Not that Jerry would take it all: he had some small measure of integrity, as in very small.

He'd told the bloke it was imperative that they should meet up. Jerry had come into some information about the bloke's mate, and he felt it his duty to pass it on to prevent the mate landing in big trouble.

The pub was anonymous, frosted glass on the tap room window, the place crawling with drinkers and buzzing with conversation behind a perpetual cloud of pipe and cigarette smoke, making it difficult to see as far as the next table. Jerry lit up a Tom Thumb cigar and ordered a half of mild.

He was never a big drinker, preferred to keep his wits about him. You never knew when you'd need to get out of somewhere quick.

He'd clocked his quarry through the haze. A man alone, looking out of place and uncomfortable: the only person in the pub wearing a suit. Jerry had noticed the newish Vauxhall Cresta parked on the road outside and wondered if it might be his.

He swaggered over and placed his hat on the table. "Mind if I join you, squire?" Whether or not, Jerry had already taken a seat, setting down his beer and crossing his legs.

His quarry was a miserable-looking geezer, a sort of haunted look about his long, pale, bearded face and mean little mouth. He stared back at Jerry.

"Are you the bloke who -?"

"That's me, squire. And you'll have good reason to be grateful to me. Leastways, your mate will."

The man shifted uncomfortably in his seat. "I don't know what you mean. Who are you?"

Jerry wasn't answering that last one. Instead, he sat at his ease, puffing peacefully away at his little cigar.

"Used to drop into the Blue Dahlia in Oxford once upon a time, didn't you?"

"Blue Dahlia?"

"A night club off St Clements."

The man shrugged. "Can't say I know it."

Jerry Rudd sighed. "Don't piss me around, squire," he said wearily. "I've seen you there and I don't forget a face."

"Okay. Maybe I went there once or twice, but that was a while ago. I don't go near Oxford these days."

Jerry Rudd grinned smugly. "See – told you. Minute I set eyes on you the other day, I remembered where I'd seen you. Not much gets past me."

The man was looking agitated. "But – how did you track me down?"

"Oh, ways and means," Jerry replied enigmatically. "Ways and means."

"Please – will you tell me what this is all about? I really do need to get home."

"No need to get jumpy, squire. You'll remember Colin Trevis, won't you?"

"Who?"

"Oh, heck. Big bloke, reckoned he was God's gift. He's dead now, but he was at the Dahlia the night I clapped eyes on you. He was often there, selling things on to young 'uns like yourself."

"Not to me, he didn't. I've got a responsible job. I don't go anywhere near drugs."

"Look, squire." Jerry was working hard to remain patient. "This isn't about you and it's not about drugs. It's about your mate. The one you were with at the Dahlia. Any chance you might remember him?"

The man seemed oblivious to the sarcasm: he was a real bundle of fun and no mistake. "I see him from time to time. Not often, these days. In fact, hardly at all. I've moved on from there."

"He sounded a right cocky little so-and-so that time I was there. You'll remember that Col Trevis sold him a gun?"

"Look, what *is* this about? I can't hang around here. I need to be on my way."

He pushed back his chair and started to get up. Rudd was amazed at how on edge he was. But he hadn't finished with him – not by a long way – and peremptorily waved him back into his seat.

"Squire, this isn't going away." *Not now I've got a handle on it, it won't,* Jerry was thinking. "Your pal could be in big trouble. All I'm asking is that you pass this on to him. Listen, there's this cop named Gallian at Oxford nick. He left the force after he got wounded in a shooting. He's back now, in CID, and I can tell you he's no mug. From what I hear, it won't be long before he's on to your mate, and I reckon you ought to tip him off – after all, that's what mates are for, ain't it? Let him know he needs to get his story straight before Gallian catches up with him."

"Yeah, alright." The man's agreement was grudging. "I – I'll see him. Leave it with me, right? Good of you to tell me. Well – I ought to get on."

Jerry studied the man closely. He was puzzled. He'd never come across anyone so jumpy. Blimey, the bloke was shaking like a leaf, finishing his drink in such a hurry, that it was spilling out of the glass and dribbling down the front of his shirt.

Unless of course, *he* was the one who'd bought the gun off Trevis, not his mate. Although as Jerry Rudd recalled it, this geezer had hardly said a word. It was his mouthy mate who'd been making all the noise.

He stretched out a hand as the man got to his feet. "Er, squire, before you go?"

"What?"

"I've come out of my way to meet up with you tonight. Train travel's not cheap. Be nice if you could spare me something for my trouble – by way of appreciation, like. Dare say your mate'll be so grateful when you tip him off, he'll see you right."

The man dithered, wanting to run away but lacking the courage. He fumbled in an inside pocket, brought out a shiny leather wallet, nearly dropped it and fished about in it for a note.

He dragged out a fiver. "This is all I've got till I get paid Friday," he mumbled wretchedly.

"Friday'll soon come round," Jerry reassured him easily, as he gently prised it from the man's grasp. He glanced at it dismissively. Looked like he'd be buying another platform ticket on the way home. Still, five bars were better than nothing.

And better still, Rudd realised that this gloomy geezer had something to hide. He wouldn't have got so het up over the fate of a man he hadn't seen for ages. So, it hadn't been a wasted evening after all. Full of Eastern promise, as the TV ad said.

"Listen," the man was whining, "that's it now, okay? I'll pass the information on. But I don't see him much anymore, and so don't contact me again, d'you hear? I don't want anything more to do with this."

Jerry Rudd nodded treacherously and watched his quarry go, almost tripping over a chair in his hurry to get away.

"You've got problems, squire," he murmured, as he stuffed the fiver into his coat pocket. "And I can guarantee you'll end up paying more than this. After all, I know where to find you."

24

Neal gathered Jill up in his arms. Sally, watching from the doorway, felt quite moved. Taff Thomas, Paul Hodgson and the uniformed sergeant, whose name she later learned was Tomkins, stood behind her on the landing, and if not for their burly presence she might have shed a tear. No-one spoke, but words would have been out of place, and there was nothing any of them could possibly contribute.

Neal sank down on to the dressing table stool, holding Jill close, lovingly stroking her face, her hair.

"Never had you down as a cricketer." His voice was a croak, overburdened with emotion.

"Didn't think you would." Jill's words came out jerkily, and he could tell she was on the verge of tears. Her voice was muffled as she laid her head against his chest. "But Uncle Lam still turns out for Braxbury's 3rd XI, and someone has to face his off spin when he needs to practise."

Thomas and Hodgson came forward, easing their way past Sally. Taff grabbed Alton by the shoulders and hauled him upright, while Paul Hodgson cuffed his hands behind his back, taking care not to be too gentle and forcing the convict to cry out. He was still groggy, and Taff delivered a sharp slap to the side of his face to bring him round.

Stung, Alton let fly a volley of colourful abuse, although he seemed to have no idea of the meaning of half of the random epithets he'd probably picked up in prison.

His captors were unimpressed. "Watch your foul mouth," Taff growled. "There are ladies present."

"He's just showing off," Paul grumbled. "And he's got nothing to show off about." He swivelled Alton roughly round to face the door and propelled him out on to the landing. But the convict's anger was spent. He nodded towards Jill, an expression of something like awe on his grubby, unshaven face.

"Who the heck does she reckon she is?" he gasped. "Ruddy Ted Dexter?"

The two constables didn't wait for an answer. "We'll find you a nice, uncomfortable cell for the night, boyo," Taff promised him. "You can count on it." Turning in the doorway, he assured Neal they'd call Uncle Tom to let him know they were bringing him in, and that Jill was, thankfully, unharmed.

Once they'd gone, Tomkins went off to make sure the house was secure, while Sally went down to the kitchen to brew them all some tea. Left alone with Neal, Jill found her voice.

As Alton had placed his hand over her mouth, stifling her scream, Jill had smelt his rancid, rasping breath, felt him pressing disgustingly against her, her arms pinned helplessly to her sides. She still held on to the handle of her uncle's cricket bat, but it was useless without her being able to do something violent with it.

So, she retaliated with the only weapon left to her: she sank her teeth into the offending hand. Alton yelled, a primeval howl, and his grip was loosened.

Firming up her grip on the handle, she raised the bat as high as she could and rammed it down on to his toes. That set off another yell, louder and wilder, and suddenly she was free, with Alton staggering back into the open doorway.

Jill turned, knowing her safety – and maybe her survival – depended on acting quickly. She raised the bat and swung it round in a wide arc to clatter the blade into the side of Alton's head. He immediately fell silent, stared at her oddly, almost with indignation, his eyes wide and vacant. He tottered forward two uncertain steps and, as Jill skipped nimbly out of his way, collapsed face down across the bed.

He lay still. Jill clung to the bat, staring down at him anxiously but not wanting to get too close. The thought crossed her mind that she'd probably killed him. And then she decided she probably hadn't, that he might be faking, awaiting the right moment, so she'd have to be on her guard, ready to whack him again if he stirred.

Suddenly, she felt faint and crumpled on to her dressing table stool. Her senses were beginning to drift, the room spinning. She clung to the bat, telling herself she must remain alert in case he awoke. But, peering across at him, she could see that he still wasn't moving. She held on desperately to consciousness, until she knew her willpower was waning. Then, in the distance, she heard the sound of a police siren edging nearer, and finally she felt able to let go, floated down into a glorious, muffled darkness and dreamed of Neal entering the room, picking up the sagging rag doll and holding her in his strong and loving arms…

Right where he held her now, and Jill wished she could stay there forever.

She sat up as Sally Dakers brought in a tea tray and poured them all a cup. She persuaded Jill to take extra sugar in hers, and Jill, used to taking her tea without, decided it was a sensible suggestion and went along with it.

Tomkins came in, gratefully accepting a cup from Sally, and reported that he'd checked the house and back garden and found the summerhouse unlocked.

That brought Jill back to life. She was suddenly furious, colour flooding back to her cheeks. "So that's how he got in! I've *told* Uncle Lam time and time again not to keep a house key in the summerhouse!"

Tomkins was looking officious. "I'll be sure to speak to him, Miss Westmacott," he promised solemnly.

Jill smiled dangerously. "You won't be anywhere near as stern as I shall, Sergeant Tomkins," she declared.

"I don't doubt it, miss."

Neal was pleased to see the two of them exchange a rare smile. He was no great fan of Tomkins himself, although given the seriousness of the situation the man had gone out of his way to be helpful that evening. He wondered if Jill would look kindlier on the Braxbury sergeant in future. She'd never liked him, but at least that evening had seen something in the way of a truce.

Leaving Jill and Sally to chat over their tea, Neal went with Tomkins to seek out the key to the summerhouse, which Alton had assiduously left under the flowerpot by the door and thanked him for getting to Briar Hedge so quickly. He apologised for yelling at the sergeant on his arrival but admitted he'd been under some strain. Tomkins acknowledged that he understood: he'd known people a lot angrier.

They parted company, and Neal and Jill, after locking up the house, gave Sally a lift back to her digs. The girls seemed to have got on well together, and Jill announced her intention to invite Sally to tea when convenient, so that they could get to know one another better.

"I presume Neal will allow you to take a day off at some stage?" Jill asked pointedly.

"Once we've sorted this case, Sally," Neal replied, "I'll get Jill to contact you."

They dropped Sally off, Jill remarking how quickly she'd taken to her, and that she felt her to be a genuinely nice girl.

"She's only been working with me a few days," Neal said, "but I can see she's got the makings of a good detective too."

He'd told Jill he was taking her back to the flat and that there'd be no argument, but he could tell she felt uncertain about it.

"What will Mr and Mrs Stone think?"

"Well, I imagine they'll be in bed and asleep by now, and I'll be gone early anyway, so by the time they're up and about they'll believe you've just arrived, as you've done every day this week, to busy yourself about the flat. And in any case, Jill Westmacott, my mind's made up. You're staying at the flat, as I said before, and there'll be no argument."

They'd arrived there by then and, as he helped her out of the car, Jill, suddenly looking pale and exhausted, almost fainted into his arms. He could tell the shock of Alton's violent assault and its near consequences had just hit her. "Oh, Neal, I thought he – that he was going to -."

"But he didn't, darling. You were very brave and too resourceful for the likes of him. Now listen, I don't want you to waste any more thought on him. Taff and Paul have locked him away for the night, and tomorrow he's going back where he belongs. And he won't be coming out again for a very long time."

He walked her into the hallway and up the stairs, supporting her all the way. Once in the flat, he made more tea, adding a slug of whisky to each cup. He went and sat beside her.

"Please, Neal. Just stay here and hold me. I need to feel your arms around me. Oh, my goodness, poor Uncle Lam. He'll be so shocked when he hears…"

"I'll speak to him from the station first thing tomorrow morning," Neal promised. "Then I'll get him to phone you here."

He sat holding her, and eventually she dropped off to sleep in his arms. He picked her up and took her through to the bedroom, made sure she was comfortable and covered her with the eiderdown. As he gazed down at her peaceful face, it occurred to him how close he might have come to losing her that evening. He sat beside the bed, bowed his head and muttered his sincere thanks for her deliverance, then sat and watched her sleeping, realising his own face was moist with tears.

"I shall look after you, Jill," he vowed solemnly. "And please don't ever doubt it." He got up, closed the door on her and tried to make himself comfortable in one of the armchairs. He lay awake for some time before a deep sleep claimed him.

Jill woke him at seven, bright and cheerful, with tea, cereal and toast, declaring that she'd go back that night with her uncle. She'd lived for the last five years at Briar Hedge and had spent quite a few nights there alone. She declared pluckily that it would take more than the memory of Henry Alton to deter her.

Neal thought she was putting on a brave face and, for his own part, was determined to return to the argument later. "We'll come to some arrangement," he remarked enigmatically, as she sent him on his way to work with a kiss.

25

As soon as he arrived at the station, Neal phoned Jill's uncle at the number she'd given him that morning and informed him about what had happened the previous evening. Colonel Wilkie was understandably taken aback and promised he'd head for home immediately.

Neal told him there was no need to rush, Jill was fine, and the house secure. He gave Wilkie the telephone number for the flat, and the colonel promised to ring Jill right away. Neal went on to say that it would be best if she stayed where she was for the day. He'd bring her back to Briar Hedge that evening once Wilkie was home and settled. Privately, he'd hoped to keep Jill at the flat at least overnight, but protocol (of which Lambert Wilkie was the last word) raged against it.

That done, he oversaw the matter of transferring Henry Alton back to Grantonwood prison. A police van was waiting in the yard, and Taff Thomas and Paul Hodgson provided an escort. The convict cut a dejected figure as he was led outside. His escapade was bound sure to get him time added on to his sentence, and he was unlikely to be endangering anyone for a long while.

Naturally, Larry Rackham, a local reporter, short, persistent and a perpetual nuisance, who was always looking for a big story to sell to one of the national newspapers, had been quick to get wind of Alton's re-capture. He was down at the nick early on with a cameraman in tow, sniffing around for information. His first port of call was Tom Wrightson, impassable at the desk, from whom he got precisely nothing, except to be escorted along to the DCI's office.

Pilling hated journalists of any description, and Larry Rackham was top of his list. He grudgingly supplied the reporter with a statement, letting him continue in his mistaken belief that the convict had been apprehended *in* Braxbury, rather than outside it. His officers had acted on an anonymous tip-off, and Alton was currently languishing in a cell, awaiting transport to ferry him back to Grantonwood prison.

Apart from a photograph of a sorry-looking convict being led out to the prison van and a long wait for the said van to show up at the station, that was all Rackham managed to get, and once he'd gone, Pilling left Taff Thomas, Paul Hodgson and Sergeant Tomkins under no illusion that if any further information about the incident leaked out, they'd be held fully responsible – and they all knew what that meant. He didn't bother with Tom Wrightson, confident that any journalist making an approach to him would come up against the most solid of brick walls, and he'd had the foresight to send Mal Brady out on an errand the moment he arrived for work, as he'd sensed that a visit from Rackham or another of his ilk might not be far away. As far as Don Pilling was concerned, the Henry Alton incident was closed.

The DCI was waiting for Neal when he came back in. It was time they interviewed Trevis' cousin, Micky Parkin. Neal was aware that his guv'nor was keeping a close eye on his handling of the investigation because he was having to report to him on a daily basis to review progress. The decision to interview alongside him showed that Pilling was stepping up his interest in the case.

Tom Wrightson brought Parkin along to the interview room. The boy wasn't long out of his teens, his features pale and pinched beneath a mane of greasy dark hair. Parkin looked scared, and Neal could see that he'd been crying.

Pilling indicated that he wanted Neal to take the lead, and he began by telling the boy that he was charged with evading arrest and assaulting a police officer. "Even though it was only Brady," he heard the DCI mutter disparagingly under his breath.

Micky Parkin took this in and looked helplessly from one man to the other. He seemed about to give way to fresh tears.

"It was me," he blurted suddenly. "I can't go on pretending it wasn't. Gloria said I didn't ought to let it bother me. But it does – has done for ages…"

Pilling switched Neal a puzzled frown, but Neal was intent for the boy to go on talking. "What was it you did, Micky?" he asked gently.

"The wages snatch." Both policemen were suddenly very interested. "It was me. I got out while I could. No-one saw me, I'm sure, though Gloria said she'd give me an aller-by. And I only done it that once, honest. I was scared stiff when Col asked me, but he said I got to, there was nobody else. The geezer who helped him before, when they done those mail vans, he'd done a runner by then. I – I've no idea who he was."

Don Pilling weighed in, his voice ringing with authority. "Right, lad. Let's get this straight. You're owning up to being the third man on the wages van snatch that went wrong, when Col Trevis and Roy Gorrie were killed?"

"Yeah, that's right. But, honest, swear to God I didn't want to do it. It was Col made me. See, I'd been to bed with Gloria, and he must've got to know about it. Not that he wanted her, with him having these other women on the go, but he was going to make me suffer for it. Gloria too, 'cause I know he socked her one the night before the snatch."

"Okay, Micky," Neal said reasonably. "It's good that you've told us this. The other driver, the one who helped do the mail vans, are you sure you've no idea who he was? Anything you can give us could prove helpful."

He was alert to Pilling's sharp glance. They were both wondering if the Face might have been the missing driver.

Micky Parkin squashed the notion. "Honest, mister, I've no idea. I never saw him nor heard a name mentioned."

"So, who were Trevis' women? I know Loretta Taine was one."

"Yeah, Col was talking about ditching Gloria and marrying her. There was another one, but he never mentioned her by name. Someone new I think, 'cause he was round Loretta a lot, and he wouldn't have wanted her to find out about it."

Neal could tell the DCI was pleased. Parkin's confession had provided the penultimate missing piece in the jigsaw of the van robberies, a case going back more than two years. But Parkin wasn't done yet. His eyes, wide and soulful, were trained beseechingly on Neal's face.

"Will – will I go down, mister?"

Neal glanced at Pilling, who answered with a nod for him to go on. The DCI understood the way his mind was working.

"Probably for a short stretch, Micky," he replied. "But you can make it shorter."

If Parkin had been standing, he'd have tripped over himself. "Wh- what do I have to do?"

"You were Col Trevis' cousin, right? You went around with him a lot?"

"Yeah, I did. I sort of looked up to Col. He was good to me when my old man was inside, and my mum had run off."

"Col was often down at the Blue Dahlia, used to do a bit of buying and selling. Were you sometimes with him when he did that?"

"Yeah, yeah – sometimes."

"Let's go back to more than two years ago – November '61. Col bought a gun off a man called Arnie Skelton. You know him?"

Parkin was displaying a puppy-like eagerness to supply the right answers. "Yeah, I know Arnie. He got done for theft, but he never split on Col. He knew it'd be more than his life was worth to have done that."

"And Col sold the gun on quickly. Were you present when he did?"

The boy looked vague, his brain cells working overtime.

Pilling cut in gruffly. "We're counting on you here, lad. Help us with this, and we can help you. Might even be talking a suspended sentence. No bullshit, mind."

Parkin swallowed noisily. "He sold it on to some young bloke."

The Face's identikit picture was already out of Neal's jacket pocket.

"To him?"

Parkin studied the picture closely then shook his head. "No, not him." He looked at it some more. "But I'm sure that bloke was with him, else it was somebody like him. I think they were mates. The one who bought it, he was showing off, reckoning he was so big buying his own popgun. Col charged him way over the odds, but the stupid berk didn't know no better –

he stumped up and paid what Col asked – didn't have a clue. We nearly peed ourselves laughing about it, once him and his mate had cleared off."

"Did you hear a name?" Neal sensed the tension in his own words. "Did either of these blokes call the other by his name?"

"The bloke in the picture there – he called the one who bought it something like 'Mart' or 'Mark'. He didn't say a lot else, 'cause the one who wanted the gun never stopped yapping. But they kept grinning at each other, as if they were sharing some sort of joke."

Mark Jevons. Turning to Pilling, Neal tried to keep the eagerness out of his voice. "We need to get him here, guv. He should still be at work."

"Dakers will know where to find him, won't she? Send her and one of the uniforms – Hodgson's reliable – and fetch him in."

Neal was already at the door and sending a passing Yvonne Begley to round up his two colleagues. Then he asked Tom Wrightson to return Parkin to his cell, after reassuring him that they'd carefully consider his co-operation.

Once they'd appeared, he gave Dakers and Hodgson their instructions. "He'll be at the bank's main branch in the High Street," Dakers said and went off with Hodgson to collect Mark Jevons. They were to keep him in the interview room until Neal was ready to see him.

He went back there to find Pilling awaiting him, stern-faced.

"Jevons might lead you to him, Neal," he warned. "And then again, he might not. I don't want you blasting in to harangue him the minute they get him here. You must be patient. Have a break until he's here and had time to feel sorry for himself. It'll do no harm to let him sweat a bit."

They were wise words, and Neal took care to heed them. He fetched himself a cup of tea, returned to his office and phoned Jill. She'd spent a happy and peaceful morning at the flat. Her uncle had rung her there, and she'd given him an edited version of events to set his mind at rest. Neal promised he'd run her back to Briar Hedge after they'd had tea together that evening. Jill declared herself satisfied with the compromise.

"I told you we could come to some arrangement," he teased her.

As he rang off and replaced the receiver, his parting words seemed to resonate in his brain. He recalled that he'd spoken them to Jill earlier that morning on leaving the flat and supposed that was why they'd sounded familiar. But he was sure he'd heard them spoken by someone else.

A moment later, he had it. They were the words Doris Medway had overheard Derek speaking into the phone the night before the break-in at Ellison's gallery on the Wednesday.

Did they have some significance?

Before long, Sally Dakers looked in to say that they'd brought in Mark Jevons, who was waiting unhappily in the interview room. Neal told her something else had cropped up, and that he wouldn't be ready for a while. He instructed her to provide Jevons with some refreshment, get Paul Hodgson to keep an eye on him, then take a break herself.

Once Sally had gone, he glanced through the notes he'd jotted down in the last ten minutes.

- Derek Medway going out on the Monday evening in his everyday clothes. Meeting some mates?
- His phone call on the Tuesday, and the words *'we can come to some arrangement'*.
- Going out smartly dressed to break into the Ellisons' gallery safe on the Wednesday.
- His body found over two years later, dressed in those Wednesday clothes.
- Col Trevis, Medway's accomplice, who had in all likelihood shot him.
- Col talking about ditching Gloria for Loretta Taine.
- Micky Parkin's assertion that Trevis had another woman in his life besides Loretta.
- And the anonymous tip-off which had scuppered the wages snatch: a woman's voice – the final piece in that particular jigsaw.

Gathering together his notes as well as his thoughts, Neal went along the corridor and knocked on the DCI's door.

26

Don Pilling lit his pipe and patiently heard Neal out. Through the haze, Neal could see how hard he was concentrating. Once he'd finished speaking, Pilling rested his pipe in the ashtray and stared keenly at his DS.

"It's a long shot, lad."

"But aren't we into long shots, Guv?"

"Yes, but unless there's a confession, I can't see us making any of it stick."

"It'll at least clear Derek Medway's name of murder."

"Medway was a cheat, a villain, a lowlife…"

Neal knew the DCI was testing him because he was more fair-minded than that.

"And no murderer," Neal replied firmly. "It'll be some consolation for his mother to know that."

Pilling pushed back his chair and got to his feet. "Pass my hat and coat, then, Sergeant." He grinned tightly as Neal handed them over. "Let's go and give this a try."

Neal could tell his boss was taking this seriously, rather than simply giving free rein to his hunch, when Pilling decided they'd take the more official-looking Wolseley and get WPC Begley to drive them. He also instructed Yvonne to accompany them into the house. It was a good ploy, putting them on the front foot: the big car and a uniformed presence were enough to put the wind up anyone who had something to hide. As a bonus, when they got there, the Cortina stood on the drive alongside the little A40. Neal was pleased that Dale Corlett should be present.

Nadine Ellison answered the door. Mid-afternoon, and she was wrapped in a blue-and-white kimono which suggested she was wearing nothing or very little underneath. Her expression was the far side of welcoming.

"Your timing leaves much to be desired," she rebuked Neal archly, then nodded dismissively at Pilling, scruffy in his rumpled raincoat and battered trilby. "And who's this?" She didn't comment on Yvonne: the uniform was a big enough clue to her identity.

Pilling answered for himself, as Neal knew he would, in his gruff, no-nonsense voice. "Detective Chief Inspector Pilling, Mrs Ellison. And this is a murder inquiry. May we come in?"

"It's hardly convenient," Nadine protested haughtily.

"Murder seldom is," Pilling declared drily. "But we can stand and discuss it here, if you prefer, for the benefit of your neighbours."

Nadine's reply was to tug the door back sulkily, a gesture which reminded Neal of Gloria Trevis. She flounced ahead of them into the sitting room, leaving Yvonne to close the door. They followed her to find Dale Corlett, clad in a white towelling dressing gown, lounging in an armchair. Two martinis stood eloquently on the coffee table.

On catching sight of Neal and his entourage, Corlett leapt to his feet in outrage, his face colouring. "What the devil do you mean by barging in here -?"

Neal waved him back into his seat. "And good afternoon to you, Mr Corlett. We didn't barge in – Mrs Ellison admitted us. You won't have met Detective Chief Inspector Pilling, and that's WPC Begley. I'm glad to find you present."

Corlett fell back into his chair, embarrassed and angry. "This is becoming harassment," he said waspishly. "Perhaps I should call your solicitor, Nadine?"

"Perhaps later," the DCI replied enigmatically. He and Neal remained standing, as Nadine Ellison went over to perch on the arm of Corlett's chair, defiantly sampling her martini and avoiding eye contact with everyone.

Pilling signalled for Yvonne Begley to come into the room and close the double doors.

"You should calm down, Mr Corlett," he went on reasonably. "None of this may affect you directly. It's Mrs Ellison we've come to see.

DS Gallian has some questions he'd like to ask regarding the murder of Derek Medway."

"Are you implying that I was involved in it?" Nadine snapped.

"No-one's implying anything." The embodiment of reason, Pilling might have been her favourite uncle and Nadine the importunate niece. "But it's something you need to hear, Mrs Ellison."

He nodded to Neal, who cleared his throat and launched in. "Let's just run back over what we've assumed so far. Derek Medway robbed the gallery safe. His accomplice was Colin Trevis, who'd been working at the house and had got to know the layout. The robbery took place on Wednesday 22nd November '61, and Medway was caught in the act by Bernard Ellison. Medway killed Mr Ellison, and then was himself killed by Trevis, when they discovered the haul from the safe was nowhere near what they'd expected."

Corlett was on his feet again in an effort to justify his existence. Neal noticed that the legs which protruded from beneath the dressing gown, though beautifully bronzed, were rather spindly.

"We've already agreed that's what happened," Corlett stormed. "Why do you need to come back here to tell us something we already know?"

Neal ignored him, turning to Nadine. "Mrs Ellison, Trevis worked here during the September and October of that year. Would you say he was fully informed about the comings and goings of yourself and your husband?"

She was struggling to contain her impatience. "As I told you before, Sergeant, Colin Trevis became very friendly with my poor husband. I don't think there was much that Bernard kept from him. To be fair, neither of us realised at that time that he was a snake in the grass."

"So, if he knew your husband's habits, for instance that he went out every Monday evening to his club, why would he arrange for Medway to break in on the Wednesday when Mr Ellison was likely to be at home?"

Neal had to admire Nadine Ellison's poise. There was hardly a moment's hesitation before she answered.

"I was going out. I expect Trevis assumed that Bernard would go with me."

"Yet when he was out on Mondays, by your own admission you were out too, more often than not."

"Not always. And this is all beginning to sound too much like speculation, Sergeant Gallian."

"Maybe, Mrs Ellison. "But it's a theory – no more than that."

She gave back his stare, but he wasn't going to be the first to flinch away. He'd admired her coolness under pressure but now understood it was more a coldness. She was a superior type of woman, used to getting her own way, heartlessly ambitious. He wondered if Dale Corlett realised that he was not so much a lover as an acolyte, solely there at her whim and to do her bidding. Neal wouldn't have liked to guess at her reaction if she found out that Corlett was dallying with Loretta Taine. If and when she did, Corlett would have to take his chance, and it was bound to be a slim one. Perhaps he should get out while the going was good, but Neal wasn't about to suggest it.

He ploughed on. "When Derek Medway went out on the Monday evening, his mother told me he was wearing scruffy, everyday clothes. 'Off to meet some mates' was his explanation.

"On the Tuesday evening, she overheard him making a phone call. "We can come to some arrangement" were the words he used. Who might he have been phoning?

"On the Wednesday evening, he was dressed smartly. He was wearing those same clothes when we discovered his body last week. Smart clothes for a break-in?

"What I'm thinking, Mrs Ellison, is that Medway robbed your husband's safe on the Monday evening. He didn't find a lot of money but found something else: the plans for the wages snatch. And on the Wednesday, he was meeting whoever he'd phoned the previous evening – 'to come to some arrangement' – presumably a financial one.

"He was often hanging around Col Trevis. But I don't believe Trevis was his accomplice. Medway was used to operating alone, and I believe it was a tip-off from Trevis which put him up to the burglary. I believe, too, that your husband may have been involved."

Corlett was on his feet again, enraged. "Bernard involved in the wages snatch? Sergeant, this must stop. It's a preposterous suggestion!" He turned to Pilling. "You're his superior," he stormed. "Aren't you going to do anything about this?"

Pilling steadfastly ignored the outburst, and Neal found himself wondering how well Corlett might have known Bernard Ellison, or if, in fact, they'd ever met. He treated the interruption with the contempt it merited.

"Col Trevis organised the wages snatch," he went on. "He was friendly with Mr Ellison, and I'm sure the plans were in Mr Ellison's safe. That suggests collusion somewhere."

"Oh, that's utterly ridiculous!" Nadine turned away, her face a mask of fury.

"You knew Colin Trevis well, Mrs Ellison?" Don Pilling cut in smoothly, and Neal noticed the sharp glance Dale Corlett directed at her.

Nadine was ice-cold now. "As I told your sergeant – Trevis forced his attentions upon me."

"You weren't having an affair with him?" The DCI's tone was one of polite inquiry.

"Most certainly not! How *dare* you suggest it?"

Pilling went on, unperturbed. "Yet a witness recently told us that Trevis was involved with more than one woman. The one we know about was Loretta Taine. Trevis had talked of divorcing his wife and marrying her. Who might this other woman have been - because it certainly wasn't Gloria Trevis?"

Neal swept in before Nadine could form a stinging retort. "I'm thinking Derek Medway might have phoned your husband on the Tuesday to sort out an arrangement, because he'd found the plans when he'd robbed the safe. It would make sense for him to have been *invited* along for the Wednesday evening to discuss terms, hence the smarter clothes. And that was the evening when Col Trevis staged the robbery, killed Mr Ellison, then probably knocked out Medway, making sure to leave his tell-tale fingerprints, before taking him off to a lonely spot to shoot him and dispose of his body. I can't believe a villain of Derek Medway's experience would have left a convenient set of prints on a glass and decanter.

"Trevis knew Medway had got hold of the plans. So, why not deal with him directly and silence him? Unless the prime objective in all this was the murder of Bernard Ellison?"

He held up a silencing hand as Nadine opened her mouth to protest. "Oh, there's more, Mrs Ellison. Three weeks after your husband's murder, Colin Trevis was killed in that same wages snatch which went wrong. It went wrong because the police received an anonymous phoned tip-off from a woman. Perhaps a woman scorned by Trevis? Someone who knew where and when the ambush would take place, someone who maybe had even planned it with him?"

Nadine Ellison remained cold and contemptuous, determined not to give way to anger. Dale Corlett sat watching her with awe and perhaps a little fear.

"Highly likely, Sergeant, the woman who tipped off your people was Trevis' long-suffering wife. Or possibly the Taine woman. I doubt if Trevis would have gone so far as to marry a woman like her. Dale!" she snapped. "Pass me the telephone. I'm contacting my solicitor now."

Pilling stretched out a hand to forestall him. "You're over-reacting, Mrs Ellison. Be advised that no-one's placing you under arrest or even conducting a formal interview. As DS Gallian has said, what you've heard is no more than a theory. But of course, any further help you can give us would be greatly appreciated."

He signalled to Yvonne Begley to open the doors into the hallway. "We'll see ourselves out," he concluded pleasantly. "Good afternoon, Mrs Ellison, Mr Corlett." He turned and led the way out of the house.

Neal's parting glimpse of Nadine and Corlett was of the pair of them looking stunned and staring after the departing police contingent open-mouthed.

He rather thought that his theory might have ruined their afternoon.

27

On their return to the station, Pilling led Neal straight to his office and pointed him to a seat, as he hung up his hat and raincoat and began stuffing tobacco into the bowl of his pipe. He grinned: something few of his colleagues regularly witnessed.

"Spot on, Neal," he said. "For my money, Ellison's bitchy comment about Loretta Taine gave her away. But we'll never pin it on her. Everyone else who was involved is dead. She got rid of her husband to inherit his house and money. For all we know – and it's my guess it could well be the case – Bernard Ellison may have been completely innocent. Nadine and Trevis might well have planned the robberies together and simply used Bernard's safe to secrete their plans. And once he'd served his purpose, she got rid of Trevis, who'd two-timed her with Loretta Taine. Oh, she's as guilty as sin in my book." He chuckled softly. "I'd wager lover boy's going to be looking over his shoulder from now on, especially if, as you say, he's got something going with the Taine woman. Wouldn't like to guess at Madam Ellison's reaction if she finds out.

"I shall be keeping a close eye on Mr Corlett. Sam Diamond ran a tight ship at the Dahlia, but we've always suspected there was something going on. I have a feeling Corlett may not be so careful. And it might be worth taking a look at the lovely Nadine's finances. 'Lady Luck', isn't it? In Queen Street. I'll put out some feelers, find out how it's faring. At least we can leave that pair in no doubt that they're under scrutiny."

Neal stirred in his chair. "I'd better get along and interview Mark Jevons," he said. "He's been kicking his heels for a while."

"He'll keep a bit longer." Pipe belching out smoke which threatened to engulf the room, Pilling was in an expansive mood. "Haul Dakers in here. Let's have a word with her first."

Neal found Sally Dakers in his office and led her along to the DCI. Pilling asked how Jevons had reacted when she and Hodgson had turned up at his bank.

"I honestly thought he was going to faint, sir," Sally replied. "In fact, when we informed the manager why we were there, he was speechless. "One of my most trusted employees," he finally managed to gasp. All his colleagues looked in shock, they couldn't believe what was happening. Jevons didn't know where to look, as we led him away. And he was in tears in the car, saying he'd done nothing wrong, and if he ever did anything dishonest, he'd lose his job. He kept asking what he was supposed to have done, and all I could say was that he'd find out in due course."

Neal could tell that Sally felt Mark Jevons was innocent. For himself, he wasn't so sure.

"Want me to sit in on the interview, Neal?" Pilling asked.

Neal fought for a diplomatic answer. Personally, he felt the DCI's brooding presence would reduce the young man to a gibbering wreck.

"I'd like Dakers to interview with me, if you don't mind, Guv. She's done all the leg work on this."

Pilling was grinning again: Christmas seemed to have come early, in fact several Christmases. "Think I'd be unsympathetic, do you, Sergeant?" he asked.

"Not at all, Guv. But as I say..."

"Your point's valid." He turned to Sally. "You've worked hard on this, Dakers, and it's not gone unnoticed. DS Gallian's right: you should be there to see this through. Get along, the pair of you."

Sally was beaming. "Thank you, sir."

Neal led the way to the interview room. He felt that Jevons had to be their man but as they entered, his first impression was that he might have been wrong. "Any trouble?" he asked Paul Hodgson, who'd been keeping Jevons company.

"Got to be kidding, Gally," Hodgson grinned, as he took his leave.

Jevons looked up from where he sat at the table in the drab, comfortless interview room. From beneath a shock of mousey-brown hair which had flopped listlessly over one eye, he looked pale and wretched, his once smart brown suit creased and seeming to hang off him. Could this really be the loud-mouthed boaster who'd confidently bought the gun from Trevis? Neal found he was beginning to share Dakers' misgivings.

Neal sat, introduced them both and began the interview. By way of a test, he brought out a pack of cigarettes from his pocket, not that he smoked often and anticipating that would become not at all under Jill's future guidance. He offered the pack to Jevons, who shook his head.

"No, thank you."

"Prefer *Guards*, do you?"

"No, I – I don't smoke. I never have."

Neal shared a look with Sally. "Very wise," he said. He waited a moment for Jevons to look up and make eye contact, saw fear and hopelessness there. Because he'd been caught? Because he'd let his parents and employer down? Or because it had happened so long ago that he'd felt safe?

"You had an aunt in Rose Hill," Neal went on. "A Miss Wayfleet?"

"Y-yes. Aunt Honoria. She died last month."

"You used to visit her?"

"Occasionally."

"How long since you started going to see her? Two years?"

"More like two and a half."

"Did she ever give you money?"

"Now and then. A little. Although that wasn't why I went to see her. More out of duty, really. She was always kind when I was a child."

His mouth twitched in a nervous grin. Neal could see he was gaining a little confidence now that it appeared that he wasn't about to be subjected to the third degree. "Aunt Honoria kept her money in a tin under the bed. I offered to open a bank account for her, but she didn't trust the banks and told me roundly that she wasn't changing her habits for me or for anyone."

Neal returned Mark Jevons' nervous smile in an attempt to put him at his ease.

"What time of day did you used to visit your aunt, Mr Jevons?"

"Usually in the evenings after work."

"With your cousin?"

Jevons frowned. "Who? Terry? No, we -er, don't have a lot in common."

"Did Terry used to visit her too?"

"He said he did. Evenings, like me. His mum must have suggested it. She knew I was going there, so I dare say she'd have encouraged him to do the same."

Neal was getting the impression that the two cousins were poles apart and there wasn't much love lost between them. It didn't surprise him.

"Let's go back to round about the time when you both started to visit Miss Wayfleet," he said. "Did you ever get along to the Blue Dahlia about then?"

"Isn't that some sort of night club?"

"Just off St Clements. Know it?"

"I know of it, although I've never been there. I go out to a pub occasionally or for a meal with colleagues from the bank, but never to a night club."

"Have you ever met a man called Colin Trevis?"

Jevons thought for a moment. "No – not to my recollection."

"Or anyone who offered to sell you a gun?"

"A *gun*?" Jevons looked astonished. "Why would I want a gun? I wouldn't know what to do with it."

Neal was coming to the same conclusion himself. Again, he exchanged a look with Sally: they both knew they were heading down the wrong road. Neal cleared his throat and decided to enlighten Mark Jevons, who was looking extremely confused. That made three of them.

"Mr Jevons, we brought you here because we received information that a gun was sold to a young man who said his name was Mark. The gun was used in a series of hold-ups on corner shops a couple of years back. One of these shops was quite close to where your aunt lived."

Jevons looked lost. "But it – it wasn't me, Sergeant. I – I mean, I simply wouldn't do anything like that…"

Neal held up a placating hand. "Okay, let's try and clear this up. Dakers, would you ask Sergeant Wrightson to bring Micky Parkin in here, please?"

Sally nodded and left the room. On her return, Tom appeared with Parkin in tow, and Mark Jevons turned in his seat to stare at him. From Parkin's blank look and Jevons' increasing confusion, he saw plainly that the two young men didn't recognise one another.

"Micky, we need your help," Neal said. "We talked about Col Trevis selling a gun to a man calling himself Mark. Is this the man? Take a good look at him."

Parkin immediately shook his head. "No, not him. It was a bigger bloke."

"Mr Jevons, can you describe your cousin?"

"Er – yes. Tall – taller than me. Dark hair, well-built, talks a lot – sort of permanent insolent grin…"

Neal turned back to Parkin. "Well?"

"Sounds like him. It certainly wasn't this bloke."

"Thanks, Micky. That's a great help. You can take him back, Tom."

Once they'd gone, Neal turned back to Mark Jevons, who was shaking his head sadly. "It's not the first time Terry's done that," he said. "A while ago, he bought a record player on the never-never, pretended he was me. The shop chased me for payment and, of course, when I swore I knew nothing about it, threatened to call in the police. Mum was livid and got on right away to Aunt Joan, who got Terry to own up to it and made him pay for it out of his savings. It was all very embarrassing, and he kept saying he'd only intended it to be a joke. But it wasn't funny at the time."

"I can understand that, Mark, and I'm sorry for what you've been through today. We'll get someone to run you home. WDC Dakers will telephone your bank now and set everything right with your manager. It's been a case of mistaken identity, and we apologise for it. Just one thing, though. I must ask you to say nothing to your cousin about this. We'll be speaking to him very shortly."

Mark Jevons said he was fine with that and offered a damp hand, which Neal shook. Sally went off and came back with Yvonne Begley, who'd give their erstwhile suspect a lift home and explain the situation to his mother without mentioning Terry Arden's name.

Meanwhile, Neal reported on the outcome of the interview to DCI Pilling.

"Terry Arden's our man, Guv," he concluded. "And Micky Parkin helped us out just now in identifying him. We should bear his co-operation in mind."

"Noted, DS Gallian. I'll make sure we speak up for him. Now go and bring in your man."

28

Taking Dakers with him, he drove to Terry Arden's house in Marston. Their knock at the door was answered by Terry's mother, looking apprehensive. As she'd met her the previous day, Neal let Sally take the lead.

"Good evening, Mrs Arden. WDC Dakers, Oxford CID, and this is Detective Sergeant Gallian. You'll remember that I called yesterday. Is your son Terry in? We'd like a word with him."

"No, dear. I'm afraid he's gone off out again. Came in from work, gobbled up his tea, then said he was off to play darts."

"Do you know where we can find him?"

"A pub called the Ship & Anchor. It's somewhere out in the sticks, but I've no idea where. They travel all over the county. But Terry plays for the Rose & Crown, down the road from here. The landlord there'll know where they've gone."

Dakers was looking blank, but Neal said he knew where to find the Ship & Anchor. "It's out the other side of Woodstock," he said, then turned to Terry's mother. "Mrs Arden, I believe you recently lost your aunt – a Miss Wayfleet?"

"Aunt Honoria, yes. She passed away last month."

"Did Terry used to visit her?"

"Oh yes, he used to go quite often. Bless him, he was devoted to her."

"Did he ever receive gifts of money from his aunt?"

"Oh, I should think so. The dear soul was so generous to him. But then, she was very well off – and kept it all in a box under her bed, Terry told me. Hopefully, once the solicitor's sorted it out, it'll be shared between my sister and me, because we're about her only living relatives." Her face suddenly clouded with suspicion. "Here, Terry's not being accused of anything, is he?"

"We just need to ask him a few questions," Neal replied enigmatically. "We're very grateful for your help, Mrs Arden."

Darkness was falling as they pulled into the car park in front of the Ship & Anchor. The pub was on a lonely country road but was proving popular that evening. Only the steady *thunk* of darts punctuated the deep hum of conversation, as Neal and Sally made their way inside, shouldering through a crowd with pint glasses in their fists and cigarettes and pipes churning out such a thick curtain of smoke as to give the DCI's office the atmosphere of a studio on a health farm. Heads turned to register this invasion by official-looking strangers, and Sally's tall figure excited much interest.

Neal headed over to the dartboard, showed his warrant card and asked if Terry Arden was with them that evening?

"Well, he was," the darts team captain, a jovial barrel of a man, laughed. "But he hopped off not twenty minutes ago. Somebody phoned him in here, and he's gone off to meet 'em up in the woods across the road. He was very secretive about it, but knowing young Terry it's bound sure to be some bird. Just as well we only got him down tonight as reserve. Doubt if we'll see much more of him before closing time."

This brought a blast of merriment from the rest of the team, but Neal didn't join in. Alarm bells were ringing. He thanked the captain, and he and Sally forced their way back outside.

"You're worried, Sarge," Sally said, as the outer door swung shut behind them.

"That's right," he replied. "I'm not liking this at all. Come on, Sally. Let's try to find him."

The only lights were from the pub, a subdued glow through the misted windows, and before going any further Neal fetched a torch from the car. Across the road, a cart track with a hedge on either side climbed towards a mass of woodland. As they walked up it, the thin beam of the torch steering their way, they became aware of a faint, gasping sound, as if someone was fighting for breath. The sound grew louder, and then a silhouette lurched out of the darkness to come stumbling down the track.

Neal quickened his pace, heading towards the figure, a man, now groaning, almost doubled over with pain and clutching his chest. From above them came the sudden, violent eruption of an engine. Sally, some yards behind, yelled, "*Sarge! Look out!*" as headlights blazed in their faces.

Neal was within a few feet of the approaching figure. With the car almost upon them, he launched himself forward, losing the torch in the process and propelled himself and the tottering figure into the hedge.

As they fell, some instinct, born of his police training, made him look towards the car. It was for no more than a split second, hardly even a glimpse, scarcely enough to properly register the face, white and terrified behind the wheel, flashing past, there and then gone so quickly that it might have been no more than a trick of the imagination.

A face he knew…

A face he could never forget…

"Sally!" he bawled. "Are you alright?"

As the car roared away, eaten up by the night, he became aware of a gangling figure emerging from somewhere in the opposite hedge, snatching at pieces of twigs and leaves which had clung to her person.

"Sarge? I'm okay. What about you?"

"I'm fine. He isn't."

As he gently separated himself from the man who lay prone beneath him, Neal felt a warm wetness seeping through his coat, saw the stain spreading across it, blacker than the darkness.

Sally stood dithering on the track. "Get back to the pub," he rapped. "Phone for an ambulance – it's urgent – life and death. Go on, Sally, move!"

He heard her set off down the track, then fished around for the torch but couldn't find it. As carefully as he was able, he pulled the man clear of the hedge and laid him out on the track, tilting his head to one side. The man's breath came in slow, feeble gasps.

"Are you Terry Arden?" Neal knelt beside him, his face inches away, close enough to see the blood bubbling on his lips. He peeled off his coat, pressed it hard against the man's chest to try to stem the flow.

The man was trying to speak but couldn't form the words.

"Just nod," Neal instructed him. "You're Terry Arden?"

Yes.

"Hang in there, Terry. I'm a police officer. Help's on its way. Terry, listen, over two years ago, you visited the Blue Dahlia in Oxford. You bought a gun. A friend was with you at the time. Was he the man who attacked you here tonight?"

Arden was fast losing consciousness, his nod almost indistinct.

Yes.

Neal placed his ear close to Arden's mouth, alert to the desperation, the quiet shriek of despair in his own voice.

"Did you pass the gun on to your friend? When you'd done with it, did you pass it on to him – the man who attacked you tonight?"

He waited. The response, when it finally came, was so weak. Was it a yes, or no? It had to be yes. *He needed it to be yes.*

"I need his name, Terry. Just whisper it – whisper it..."

No response.

"Hold on, Terry. Please – it's so important you hold on. We have to find this man. Help's on its way. It won't be long now."

Two sets of hurrying footsteps sounded on the road, then on the track. Sally Dakers loomed out of the darkness, following the beam of a torch she'd borrowed from the pub. "Ambulance will be here very soon, Sarge."

"Sally." Still the desperation in his voice, its hopelessness more pronounced in his own hearing. "Did you get anything at all on that car – the make, anything at all from the number plate?"

"Nothing. I'm sorry. I was too busy getting out of the way."

"Me too. But I got the briefest glimpse of the driver."

"You recognised him. Was it -?"

"Yes. It was him."

"You're sure? You mean it was the man who -?"

"Yes. There's no way I could have been mistaken." Neal turned to the person who'd accompanied Sally from the pub, and she briefly shone the torch on his face. It was the darts team captain, his features ghastly in the glow.

"Wh-what happened?" the man gasped, as he gazed down at the dark shape on the ground.

Neal hadn't left off pressing his coat against Arden's wound. It was hopeless, he knew, but he had to make the effort, couldn't just let the young man bleed out.

"Terry's been stabbed," he said. "You told me he'd received a phone call?"

"Yes, back in the pub. Probably about half-an-hour ago now."

"Who took it? The landlord?"

"Yes."

"We'll have a word." Neal was sure he'd learn nothing, but it had to be done.

"Listen, is Terry -?"

"He's lost a lot of blood, and he's unconscious. It's not looking good."

"Blimey, this is a hell of a shock. Let's hope they can save him."

"Let's hope so." Neal doubted it, his words lacking conviction. He was aware that Sally had picked up on that. He couldn't see her face clearly but sensed her pity. He continued to hold his ruined coat in place, felt the young man's blood seeping through to his fingers, making them black and sticky as if with other people's sin. And perhaps his own.

As they waited in silence, they heard the squeal of the ambulance as it sped along the road. Sally went down to meet it. The crew were effortlessly efficient, men who'd dealt with blood and death countless times. As they carefully lifted Terry Arden on to a stretcher, Neal asked Dakers if she'd go with them to the hospital.

"Let me know when there's any news. I'll be at the station."

She was looking at him with concern. "Sarge, are you okay?"

He nodded curtly. He wasn't okay. He'd failed again, abysmally. He wanted to scream and shout, to shed tears of frustration. But he wouldn't, because he never had. Not once, on any of those many occasions when he'd fallen short of his father's uncompromisingly high standards.

If only he could cry now. But he wouldn't – wouldn't because it would solve nothing. It was all too late. Again.

"It's too late, Sally," he said. "He won't pull through."

"But you did your best." He was warmed by her consoling hand on his shoulder, moved by the tears he saw glistening in her eyes. "No-one can ever say that you didn't."

Too full to speak, he nodded his thanks, waited as Sally went off in the ambulance, watched until it was out of sight, before returning to the pub with the subdued darts captain to ask the landlord for anything he might be able to tell him about the phone call.

And knowing already what the answer would be.

29

It seemed a long time later when he arrived back at the station. He parked the Anglia in the yard and deposited his blood-wrecked coat in one of the bins. As he went in, both Don Pilling and Tom Wrightson looked up from where they stood at the desk. Neal learned later that Sally Dakers had phoned in once she'd arrived at the hospital to inform them what had happened, and that DS Gallian would be on his way back to the station once he'd completed his inquiries at the Ship & Anchor. That meant they knew the score and were awaiting him.

Yvonne Begley was close by, and Neal heard the DCI ask her to fetch some tea. Pilling was sympathetic. "We'll go along to my office, Neal." He set off to lead the way, opening the door and ushering Neal to a seat before taking his customary place behind the desk.

"He got to Terry Arden and silenced him, Guv," Neal explained, aware of the weariness and despondency in his voice. "He'd phoned the Ship & Anchor to arrange for Terry to meet him up in the woods there. All the landlord could tell me was that the caller gave no name, had quite a high-pitched voice and sounded nervous, thought it might have been a woman. But it wasn't, because I knew who it was. I got the briefest glimpse of him when he charged down the track in the car. It was him – the Face. Dakers is at the hospital in the hope that Arden will come round, but I reckon he's too far gone."

He sat hunched in his chair as Yvonne brought in the tea, poured and handed it out before departing. Neal took a slug of his, needing it, aware that the DCI was watching him closely.

"You did your best," Pilling said bluntly, echoing Dakers' words. "And there's a positive from today's work: you've obtained a measure of justice for Derek Medway. His mother will be satisfied with that – I sent Brady round to tell her. And you might like to know that I received a phone call from our friend Corlett after you'd left. He was the last word in respectful and, by jingo, he laid it on thick. You'll be devastated to learn, as was I, that poor Nadine is utterly distraught."

According to Dale Corlett, Nadine had that afternoon confided to him about how Colin Trevis had abused her and how Bernard Ellison had been completely under his sway. She'd suspected that something was going on, in effect that Trevis and Bernard had planned the mail van hold-ups and wages snatch. Bernard's business had been struggling until that last big sale. It had been Trevis' idea to do away with Bernard, who'd been getting increasingly jumpy, and frame Medway for his murder, ensuring that Medway wouldn't be around to answer for himself.

Medway had learned of the sale, broken into the safe and found the plans. He'd phoned Bernard in an attempt to blackmail him, Bernard had panicked, and Trevis had feared he was about to crack. Hence his master plan to kill two birds with one stone. That left poor, defenceless Nadine at Trevis' mercy. The only way she'd been able to stop him had been to tip off the police about the forthcoming wages snatch.

"Altogether an enterprising piece of fiction," Pilling concluded. "But I think we know different, Sergeant. However, we can prove nothing. I believe – as I know you do – that she was involved in an affair with Trevis, and that they planned everything together. She inherited Bernard's house and money and then decided to rid herself of Trevis with that tip-off. Whether we eventually collar her or not, I see it as a result."

Neal understood that his boss was trying to lift him, and he was about to make a grudging reply when the phone rang.

Pilling snatched up the receiver, grunted something into it and held it out towards Neal. "For you." His expression was sombre. "Dakers."

Neal took it from him. "Yes, Sally?"

"Sarge, I'm sorry. They've just pronounced Terry Arden dead. He never regained consciousness. His mum and sister are here. Do you want me to have a word with them?"

"Yes. Tell them it was some sort of quarrel, and that we're looking for the man responsible. Say that we'll keep in touch – that someone'll be round tomorrow. And then go home, Sally. Thank you. You've done well."

Neal returned the receiver to Pilling, whose stern gaze had never left his sergeant's face.

"You're absolutely sure it was him you glimpsed, Neal?"

"Positive. What I can't work out is how he got to know that we were on to Terry Arden."

"What about the car? Did you or Dakers get anything on it?"

"Nothing, Guv. It all happened too quickly."

"I'll send Tom out with Dakers tomorrow, see if we can get anything from any member of his darts team, interview the landlord again. They'll see the mother and sister too, find out who his friends were. Just in case someone'll be able to put a name to his killer."

"That's something I want to do myself, Guv."

Pilling ignored the request. "And you think we'll get anything from that?"

Neal had to admit there was always a chance, but it would be a slim one. Too slim. He shook his head. "I doubt it. But listen, Guv, I want to see this through. I've been with it from the beginning. It's only right that -."

"Hhmm, I doubt it too. Still, we have to go through the motions. However, it's academic as far as you're concerned, because you're off the case."

Neal had seen it coming and was quickly out of his seat. "But Guv, you can't!"

Pilling's expression was set in stone. "You've admitted yourself that we're at a dead end, and there are other matters that need looking into. I want you to go home now, Sergeant. The case – for you – is closed."

"Oh, Guv, *please* -."

"Closed, DS Gallian. You're off it. You and Dakers have worked yourselves hard these last few days. Go home – that's an order. I don't want to set eyes on you before Monday. If I do, there'll be trouble. Spend some time with Jill. She's been through a heck of an ordeal herself, and she could do with you being around for her. Next week, you'll be working something new – I'll make sure of it."

Pilling could see another protest about to erupt and curtailed it with an implacable stare. "An order, Neal. Don't make me angry."

Neal pushed back his chair and got up. "Guv." He walked slowly out and down the corridor towards the desk, aware that the DCI was watching from the doorway. Yvonne and Tom Wrightson were at the desk as he passed. Yvonne smiled sympathetically, while Tom acknowledged him with a dour nod. Tom, out of everyone there, knew what the events of the evening had meant to him.

Beyond the desk, a slim figure sat huddled in a sheepskin coat, rising as he approached. Neal guessed Tom had phoned Jill at the flat and asked her to come there to meet him. It was the sort of thing Uncle Tom would do for any of his lads and lasses.

And despite himself, Neal felt a rush of pride. He was doing the job he wanted among colleagues he liked and admired, several of whom he'd walk through fire for. And the girl he loved was greeting him with a hug and kiss, and they were walking out to the car with their arms around each other. He realised then, if he hadn't before, that Jill was his present and his future, his passport to living and reason to leave the past firmly behind – all of the past.

Unless, of course, one day…

*

The Relentless Shadow, copyright Michael Limmer 2024.

MYSTERY THRILLERS
from MICHAEL LIMMER

Michael Limmer is the author of eight mystery thrillers, of which *The Relentless Shadow* is the latest. He's also a short story writer of both mystery and Christian fiction, and all profits and royalties from the sales of his work are shared between three Christian charities. Mike's most recent novels, *The Scars of Shame* (the first in the Neal Gallian trilogy), *Marla, Past Deceiving* and the novella *Time Knows No Pity* are all available from Amazon in paperback and e-book formats.

If you've enjoyed this book, please visit Mike's website at
mikesmysteries.co.uk

*

Neal Gallian will return in

The Baited Trap

Eight months after the incident which saw the killer he knows only as 'the Face' slip from his clutches, Detective Sergeant Neal Gallian has little time to feel sorry for himself – particularly when the body of a local villain has been fished out of the canal, an MP's daughter has been abducted, and Neal finds himself walking into a bank where an armed robbery is in progress...

For more information on this and other novels featuring Neal Gallian, please visit Mike's website as listed above.